James Denney

The Atonement and the Modern Mind

James Denney

The Atonement and the Modern Mind

1st Edition | ISBN: 978-3-75237-256-4

Place of Publication: Frankfurt am Main, Germany

Year of Publication: 2020

Outlook Verlag GmbH, Germany.

THE ATONEMENT

AND

THE MODERN MIND

BY

JAMES DENNEY

PREFACE

The three chapters which follow have already appeared in *The Expositor*, and may be regarded as a supplement to the writer's work on *The Death of Christ: its place and interpretation in the New Testament*. It was no part of his intention in that study to ask or to answer all the questions raised by New Testament teaching on the subject; but, partly from reviews of *The Death of Christ*, and still more from a considerable private correspondence to which the book gave rise, he became convinced that something further should be attempted to commend the truth to the mind and conscience of the time. The difficulties and misunderstandings connected with it spring, as far as they can be considered intellectual, mainly from two sources. Either the mind is preoccupied with a conception of the world which, whether men are conscious of it or not, forecloses all the questions which are raised by any doctrine of atonement, and makes them unmeaning; or it labours under some misconception as to what the New Testament actually teaches. Broadly speaking, the first of these conditions is considered in the first two chapters, and the second in the last. The title—*The Atonement and the Modern Mind*—might seem to promise a treatise, or even an elaborate system of theology; but though it would cover a work of vastly larger scope than the present, it is not inappropriate to any attempt, however humble, to help the mind in which we all live and move to reach a sympathetic comprehension of the central truth in the Christian religion. The purpose of the writer is evangelic, whatever may be said of his method; it is to commend the Atonement to the human mind, as that mind has been determined by the influences and experiences of modern times, and to win the mind for the truth of the Atonement.

With the exception of a few paragraphs, these pages were delivered as lectures to a summer school of Theology which met in Aberdeen, in June of this year. The school was organised by a committee of the Association of Former Students of the United Free Church College, Glasgow; and the writer, as a member and former President of the Association, desires to take the liberty of inscribing his work to his fellow-students.

GLASGOW, *September* 1903.

CHAPTER I

It will be admitted by most Christians that if the Atonement, quite apart from precise definitions of it, is anything to the mind, it is everything. It is the most profound of all truths, and the most recreative. It determines more than anything else our conceptions of God, of man, of history, and even of nature; it determines them, for we must bring them all in some way into accord with it. It is the inspiration of all thought, the impulse and the law of all action, the key, in the last resort, to all suffering. Whether we call it a fact or a truth, a power or a doctrine, it is that in which the *differentia* of Christianity, its peculiar and exclusive character, is specifically shown; it is the focus of revelation, the point at which we see deepest into the truth of God, and come most completely under its power. For those who recognise it at all it is Christianity in brief; it concentrates in itself, as in a germ of infinite potency, all that the wisdom, power and love of God mean in relation to sinful men.

Accordingly, when we speak of the Atonement and the modern mind, we are really speaking of the modern mind and the Christian religion. The relation between these two magnitudes may vary. The modern mind is no more than a modification of the human mind as it exists in all ages, and the relation of the modern mind to the Atonement is one phase—it may be a specially interesting or a specially well-defined phase—of the perennial relation of the mind of man to the truth of God. There is always an affinity between the two, for God made man in His own image, and the mind can only rest in truth; but there is always at the same time an antipathy, for man is somehow estranged from God, and resents Divine intrusion into his life. This is the situation at all times, and therefore in modern times; we only need to remark that when the Atonement is in question, the situation, so to speak, becomes acute. All the elements in it define themselves more sharply. If there is sympathy between the mind and the truth, it is a profound sympathy, which will carry the mind far; if there are lines of approach, through which the truth can find access to the mind, they are lines laid deep in the nature of things and of men, and the access which the truth finds by them is one from which it will not easily be dislodged. On the other hand, if it is antagonism which is roused in the mind by the Atonement, it is an antagonism which feels that everything is at stake. The Atonement is a reality of such a sort that it can make no compromise. The man who fights it knows that he is fighting for his life, and puts all his strength into the battle. To surrender is literally to give up himself, to cease to be the man he is, and to become another man. For the modern mind, therefore, as for the ancient, the attraction and the repulsion of Christianity are concentrated at the same point; the cross of Christ is man's only glory, or it is his final stumbling-block.

What I wish to do in these papers is so to present the facts as to mediate, if possible, between the mind of our time and the Atonement—so to exhibit the specific truth of Christianity as to bring out its affinity for what is deepest in the nature of man and in human experience—so to appreciate the modern mind itself, and the influences which have given it its constitution and temper, as to discredit what is false in it, and enlist on the side of the Atonement that which is profound and true. And if any one is disposed to marvel at the ambition or the conceit of such a programme, I would ask him to consider if it is not the programme prescribed to every Christian, or at least to every Christian minister, who would do the work of an evangelist. To commend the eternal truth of God, as it is finally revealed in the Atonement, to the mind in which men around us live and move and have their being, is no doubt a difficult and perilous task; but if we approach it in a right spirit, it need not tempt us to any presumption; it cannot tempt us, as long as we feel that it is our duty. '*Who is sufficient for these things! ... Our sufficiency is of God.*'

The Christian religion is a historical religion, and whatever we say about it must rest upon historical ground. We cannot define it from within, by reference merely to our individual experience. Of course it is equally impossible to define it apart from experience; the point is that such experience itself must be historically derived; it must come through something outside of our individual selves. What is true of the Christian religion as a whole is pre-eminently true of the Atonement in which it is concentrated. The experience which it brings to us, and the truth which we teach on the basis of it, are historically mediated. They rest ultimately on that testimony to Christ which we find in the Scriptures and especially in the New Testament. No one can tell what the Atonement is except on this basis. No one can consciously approach it—no one can be influenced by it to the full extent to which it is capable of influencing human nature—except through this medium. We may hold that just because it is Divine, it must be eternally true, omnipresent in its gracious power; but even granting this, it is not known as an abstract or eternal somewhat; it is historically, and not otherwise than historically, revealed. It is achieved by Christ, and the testimony to Christ, on the strength of which we accept it, is in the last resort the testimony of Scripture.

In saying so, I do not mean that the Atonement is merely a problem of exegesis, or that we have simply to accept as authoritative the conclusions of scholars as to the meaning of New Testament texts. The modern mind here is ready with a radical objection. The writers of the New Testament, it argues,

4

were men like ourselves; they had personal limitations and historical limitations; their forms of thought were those of a particular age and upbringing; the doctrines they preached may have had a relative validity, but we cannot benumb our minds to accept them without question. The intelligence which has learned to be a law to itself, criticising, rejecting, appropriating, assimilating, cannot deny its nature and suspend its functions when it opens the New Testament. It cannot make itself the slave of men, not even though the men are Peter and Paul and John; no, not even though it were the Son of Man Himself. It resents dictation, not wilfully nor wantonly, but because it must; and it resents it all the more when it claims to be inspired. If, therefore, the Atonement can only be received by those who are prepared from the threshold to acknowledge the inspiration and the consequent authority of Scripture, it can never be received by modern men at all.

This line of remark is familiar inside the Church as well as outside. Often it is expressed in the demand for a historical as opposed to a dogmatic interpretation of the New Testament, a historical interpretation being one to which we can sit freely, because the result to which it leads us is the mind of a time which we have survived and presumably transcended; a dogmatic interpretation, on the other hand, being one which claims to reach an abiding truth, and therefore to have a present authority. A more popular and inconsistent expression of the same mood may be found among those who say petulant things about the rabbinising of Paul, but profess the utmost devotion to the words of Jesus. Even in a day of overdone distinctions, one might point out that interpretations are not properly to be classified as historical or dogmatic, but as true or false. If they are false, it does not matter whether they are called dogmatic or historical; and if they are true, they may quite well be both. But this by the way. For my own part, I prefer the objection in its most radical form, and indeed find nothing in it to which any Christian, however sincere or profound his reverence for the Bible, should hesitate to assent. Once the mind has come to know itself, there can be no such thing for it as blank authority. It cannot believe things—the things by which it has to live—simply on the word of Paul or John. It is not irreverent, it is simply the recognition of a fact, if we add that it can just as little believe them simply on the word of Jesus.[1] This is not the sin of the mind, but the nature and essence of mind, the being which it owes to God. If we are to speak of authority at all in this connection, the authority must be conceived as belonging not to the speaker but to that which he says, not to the witness but to the truth. Truth, in short, is the only thing which has authority for the mind, and the only way in which truth finally evinces its authority is by taking possession of the mind for itself. It may be that any given truth can only be reached by testimony—that is, can only come to us by some historical channel; but if it is a truth of eternal import, if it is part of a revelation of God the reception of which is eternal life, then its authority lies in itself and in its power to win the mind, and not in any witness however trustworthy.

Hence in speaking of the Atonement, whether in preaching or in theologising, it is quite unnecessary to raise any question about the inspiration of Scripture, or to make any claim of 'authority' either for the Apostles or for the Lord. Belief in the inspiration of Scripture is neither the beginning of the Christian life nor the foundation of Christian theology; it is the last conclusion—a conclusion which becomes every day more sure—to which experience of the truth of Scripture leads. When we tell, therefore, what the Atonement is, we are telling it not on the authority of any person or persons whatever, but on the authority of the truth in it by which it has won its place in our minds and hearts. We find this truth in the Christian Scriptures undoubtedly, and therefore we prize them; but the truth does not derive its authority from the Scriptures, or from those who penned them. On the contrary, the Scriptures are prized by the Church because through them the soul is brought into contact with this truth. No doubt this leaves it open to any one who does not see in Scripture what we see, or who is not convinced as we are of its truth, to accuse us here of subjectivity, of having no standard of truth but what appeals to us individually, but I could never feel the charge a serious one. It is like urging that a man does not see at all, or does not see truly, because he only sees with his own eyes. This is the only authentic kind of seeing yet known to mankind. We do not judge at all those who do not see what we do. We do not know what hinders them, or whether they are at all to blame for it; we do not know how soon the hindrance is going to be put out of the way. To-day, as at the beginning, the light shines in the darkness, and the darkness comprehends it not. But that is the situation which calls for evangelists; not a situation in which the evangelist is called to renounce his experience and his vocation.

What, then, is the Atonement, as it is presented to us in the Scriptures, and vindicates for itself in our minds the character of truth, and indeed, as I have said already, the character of the ultimate truth of God?

The simplest expression that can be given to it in words is: Christ died for our sins. Taken by itself, this is too brief to be intelligible; it implies many things which need to be made explicit both about Christ's relation to us and about the relation of sin and death. But the important thing, to begin with, is not to define these relations, but to look through the words to the broad reality which is interpreted in them. What they tell us, and tell us on the basis of an incontrovertible experience, is that the forgiveness of sins is for the Christian mediated through the death of Christ. In one respect, therefore, there is nothing singular in the forgiveness of sins: it is in the same position as every other blessing of which the New Testament speaks. It is the presence of a Mediator, as Westcott says in one of his letters, which makes the Christian religion what it is; and the forgiveness of sins is mediated to us through Christ, just as the knowledge of God as the Father is mediated, or the assurance of a life beyond death. But there is something *specific* about the mediation of forgiveness; the gift and the certainty of it come to us, not simply through Christ, but through the blood of His Cross. The sum of His relation to sin is that He died for it. God forgives, but this is the way in which His forgiveness comes. He forgives freely, but it is at this cost to Himself and to the Son of His love.

This, it seems to me, is the simplest possible statement of what the New Testament means by the Atonement, and probably there are few who would dispute its correctness. But it is possible to argue that there is a deep cleft in the New Testament itself, and that the teaching of Jesus on the subject of forgiveness is completely at variance with that which we find in the Epistles, and which is implied in this description of the Atonement. Indeed there are many who do so argue. But to follow them would be to forget the place which Jesus has in His own teaching. Even if we grant that the main subject of that teaching is the Kingdom of God, it is as clear as anything can be that the Kingdom depends for its establishment on Jesus, or rather that in Him it is already established in principle; and that all participation in its blessings depends on some kind of relation to Him. All things have been delivered to Him by the Father, and it is by coming under obligation to Him, and by that alone, that men know the Father. It is by coming under obligation to Him that they know the pardoning love of the Father, as well as everything else that enters into Christian experience and constitutes the blessedness of life in the Kingdom of God. Nor is it open to any one to say that he knows this simply because Christ has told it. We are dealing here with things too great to be simply told. If they are ever to be known in their reality, they must be revealed by God, they must rise upon the mind of man experimentally, in their awful and glorious truth, in ways more wonderful than words. They can be spoken about afterwards, but hardly beforehand. They can be celebrated and preached—that is, declared as the speaker's experience, delivered as his testimony—but not simply told. It was enough if Jesus made His disciples feel, as surely He did make them feel, not only in every word He spoke, but more emphatically still in His whole attitude toward them, that He was Himself the Mediator of the new covenant, and that all the blessings of the relation between God and man which we call Christianity were blessings due to Him. If men knew the Father, it was through Him. If they knew the Father's heart to the lost, it was through Him. Through Him, be it remembered, not merely through the words that He spoke. There was more in

Christ than even His own wonderful words expressed, and all that He was and did and suffered, as well as what He said, entered into the convictions He inspired. But He knew this as well as His disciples, and for this very reason it is beside the mark to point to what He said, or rather to what He did not say, in confutation of their experience. For it is their experience—the experience that the forgiveness of sins was mediated to them through His cross—that is expressed in the doctrine of Atonement: He died for our sins.

The objection which is here in view is most frequently pointed by reference to the parable of the prodigal son. There is no Atonement here, we are told, no mediation of forgiveness at all. There is love on the one side and penitence on the other, and it is treason to the pure truth of this teaching to cloud and confuse it with the thoughts of men whose Master was over their heads often, but most of all here. Such a statement of the case is plausible, and judging from the frequency with which it occurs must to some minds be very convincing, but nothing could be more superficial, or more unjust both to Jesus and the apostles. A parable is a comparison, and there is a point of comparison in it on which everything turns. The more perfect the parable is, the more conspicuous and dominating will the point of comparison be. The parable of the prodigal illustrates this. It brings out, through a human parallel, with incomparable force and beauty, the one truth of the freeness of forgiveness. God waits to be gracious. His pardoning love rushes out to welcome the penitent. But no one who speaks of the Atonement ever dreams of questioning this. The Atonement is concerned with a different point—not the freeness of pardon, about which all are agreed, but the cost of it; not the spontaneity of God's love, which no one questions, but the necessity under which it lay to manifest itself in a particular way if God was to be true to Himself, and to win the heart of sinners for the holiness which they had offended. The Atonement is not the denial that God's love is free; it is that specific manifestation or demonstration of God's free love which is demanded by the situation of men. One can hardly help wondering whether those who tell us so confidently that there is no Atonement in the parable of the prodigal have ever noticed that there is no Christ in it either—no elder brother who goes out to seek and to save the lost son, and to give his life a ransom for him. Surely we are not to put the Good Shepherd out of the Christian religion. Yet if we leave Him His place, we cannot make the parable of the prodigal the measure of Christ's mind about the forgiveness of sins. One part of His teaching it certainly contains—one part of the truth about the relation of God the Father to His sinful children; but another part of the truth was present, though not on that occasion rendered in words, in the presence of the Speaker, when 'all the publicans and sinners drew near to Him for to hear Him.' The love of God to the sinful was apprehended in Christ Himself, and not in what

He said as something apart from Himself; on the contrary, it was in the identity of the speaker and the word that the power of the word lay; God's love evinced itself to men as a reality in Him, in His presence in the world, and in His attitude to its sin; it so evinced itself, finally and supremely, in His death. It is not the idiosyncrasy of one apostle, it is the testimony of the Church, a testimony in keeping with the whole claim made by Christ in His teaching and life and death: '*in Him* we have our redemption, *through His blood*, even the forgiveness of our trespasses.' And this is what the Atonement means: it means the mediation of forgiveness through Christ, and specifically through His death. Forgiveness, in the Christian sense of the term, is only realised as we believe in the Atonement: in other words, as we come to feel the cost at which alone the love of God could assert itself as Divine and holy love in the souls of sinful men. We may say, if we please, that forgiveness is bestowed freely upon repentance; but we must add, if we would do justice to the Christian position, that repentance in its ultimate character is the fruit of the Atonement. Repentance is not possible apart from the apprehension of the mercy of God *in Christ*. It is the experience of the regenerate—*poenitentiam interpretor regenerationem*, as Calvin says—and it is the Atonement which regenerates.

This, then, in the broadest sense, is the truth which we wish to commend to the modern mind: the truth that there is forgiveness with God, and that this forgiveness comes to us only through Christ, and signally or specifically through His death. Unless it becomes true to us that *Christ died for our sins* we cannot appreciate forgiveness at its specifically Christian value. It cannot be for us that kind of reality, it cannot have for us that kind of inspiration, which it unquestionably is and has in the New Testament.

But what, we must now ask, is the modern mind to which this primary truth of Christianity has to be commended? Can we diagnose it in any general yet recognisable fashion, so as to find guidance in seeking access to it for the gospel of the Atonement? There may seem to be something presumptuous in the very idea, as though any one making the attempt assumed a superiority to the mind of his time, an exemption from its limitations and prejudices, a power to see over and round about it. All such presumption is of course disclaimed here; but even while we disclaim it, the attempt to appreciate the mind of our time is forced upon us. Whoever has tried to preach the gospel, and to persuade men of truth as truth is in Jesus, and especially of the truth of God's forgiveness as it is in the death of Jesus for sin, knows that there is a state of mind which is somehow inaccessible to this truth, and to which the truth consequently appeals in vain. I do not speak of unambiguous moral antipathy to the ideas of forgiveness and atonement, although antipathy to these ideas in general, as distinct from any given presentation of them, cannot but have a moral character, just as a moral character always attaches to the refusal to acknowledge Christ or to become His debtor; but of something which, though vaguer and less determinate, puts the mind wrong, so to speak, with Christianity from the start. It is clear, for instance, in all that has been said about forgiveness, that certain relations are presupposed as subsisting between God and man, relations which make it possible for man to sin, and possible for God, not indeed to ignore his sin, but in the very act of recognising it as all that it is to forgive it, to liberate man from it, and to restore him to Himself and righteousness. Now if the latent presuppositions of the modern mind are to any extent inconsistent with such relations, there will be something to overcome before the conceptions of forgiveness or atonement can get a hearing. These conceptions have their place in a certain view of the world as a whole, and if the mind is preoccupied with a different view, it will have an instinctive consciousness that it cannot accommodate them, and a disposition therefore to reject them *ab initio*. This is, in point of fact, the difficulty with which we have to deal. And let no one say that it is transparently absurd to suggest that we must get men to accept a true philosophy before we can begin to preach the gospel to them, as though that settled the matter or got over the difficulty. We have to take men as we find them; we have to preach the gospel to the mind which is around us; and if that mind is rooted in a view of the world which leaves no room for Christ and His work as Christian experience has realised them, then that view of the world must be appreciated by the evangelist, it must be undermined at its weak places, its inadequacy to interpret all that is present even in the mind which has accepted it—in other words, its inherent inconsistency—must be demonstrated; the attempt must be made to liberate the mind, so that it may be open to the impression of realities which under the conditions supposed it could only encounter with instinctive antipathy. It is necessary, therefore, at this point to advert to the various influences which have contributed to form the mind of our time, and to give it its instinctive bias in one direction or another. Powerful and legitimate as these influences have been, they have nevertheless been in various ways partial, and because of their very partiality they have, when they absorbed the mind, as new modes of thought are apt to do, prejudiced it against the consideration of other, possibly of deeper and more far-reaching, truths.

First, there is the enormous development of physical science. This has engrossed human intelligence in our own times to an extent which can hardly be over-estimated. Far more mind has been employed in constructing the great fabric of knowledge, which we call science, than in any other pursuit of men. Far more mind has had its characteristic qualities and temper imparted to it by scientific study than by study in any other field. It is of science—

which to all intents and purposes means physical science—of science and its methods and results that the modern mind is most confident, and speaks with the most natural and legitimate pride. Now science, even in this restricted sense, covers a great range of subjects; it may be physics in the narrowest meaning of the word, or chemistry, or biological science. The characteristic of our own age has been the development of the last, and in particular its extension to man. It is impossible to dispute the legitimacy of this extension. Man has his place in nature; the phenomena of life have one of their signal illustrations in him, and he is as proper a subject of biological study as any other living being. But the intense preoccupation of much of the most vigorous intelligence of our time with the biological study of man is not without effects upon the mind itself, which we need to consider. It tends to produce a habit of mind to which certain assumptions are natural and inevitable, certain other assumptions incredible from the first. This habit of mind is in some ways favourable to the acceptance of the Atonement. For example, the biologist's invincible conviction of the unity of life, and of the certainty and power with which whatever touches it at one point touches it through and through, is in one way entirely favourable. Many of the most telling popular objections to the idea of Atonement rest on an atomic conception of personality—a conception according to which every human being is a closed system, incapable in the last resort of helping or being helped, of injuring or being injured, by another. This conception has been finally discredited by biology, and so far the evangelist must be grateful. The Atonement presupposes the unity of human life, and its solidarity; it presupposes a common and universal responsibility. I believe it presupposes also such a conception of the unity of man and nature as biology proceeds upon; and in all these respects its physical presuppositions, if we may so express ourselves, are present to the mind of to-day, thanks to biology, as they were not even so lately as a hundred years ago.

But this is not all that we have to consider. The mind has been influenced by the movement of physical and even of biological science, not only in a way which is favourable, but in ways which are prejudicial to the acceptance of the Atonement. Every physical science seems to have a boundless ambition; it wants to reduce everything to its own level, to explain everything in the terms and by the categories with which it itself works. The higher has always to fight for its life against the lower. The physicist would like to reduce chemistry to physics; the chemist has an ambition to simplify biology into chemistry; the biologist in turn looks with suspicion on anything in man which cannot be interpreted biologically. He would like to give, and is sometimes ready to offer, a biological explanation of self-consciousness, of freedom, of religion, morality, sin. Now a biological explanation, when all is done, is a physical explanation, and a physical explanation of self-consciousness or the moral life is one in which the very essence of the thing to be explained is either ignored or explained away. Man's life is certainly rooted in nature, and therefore a proper subject for biological study; but unless it somehow transcended nature, and so demanded other than physical categories for its complete interpretation, there could not be any study or any science at all. If there were nothing but matter, as M. Naville has said, there would be no materialism; and if there were nothing but life, there would be no biology. Now it is in the higher region of human experience, to which all physical categories are unequal, that we encounter those realities to which the Atonement is related, and in relation to which it is real; and we must insist upon these *higher* realities, in their specific character, against a strong tendency in the scientifically trained modern mind, and still more in the general mind as influenced by it, to reduce them to the merely physical level.

Take, for instance, the consciousness of sin. Evidently the Atonement becomes incredible if the consciousness of sin is extinguished or explained away. There is nothing for the Atonement to do; there is nothing to relate it to; it is as unreal as a rock in the sky. But many minds at the present time, under the influence of current conceptions in biology, do explain it away. All life is one, they argue. It rises from the same spring, it runs the same course, it comes to the same end. The life of man is rooted in nature, and that which beats in my veins is an inheritance from an immeasurable past. It is absurd to speak of my responsibility for it, or of my guilt because it manifests itself in me, as it inevitably does, in such and such forms. There is no doubt that this mode of thought is widely prevalent, and that it is one of the most serious hindrances to the acceptance of the gospel, and especially of the Atonement. How are we to appreciate it? We must point out, I think, the consequence to which it leads. If a man denies that he is responsible for the nature which he has inherited—denies responsibility for it on the ground that it *is* inherited—it is a fair question to ask him for what he *does* accept responsibility. When he has divested himself of the inherited nature, what is left? The real meaning of such disowning of responsibility is that a man asserts that his life is a part of the physical phenomena of the universe, and nothing else; and he forgets, in the very act of making the assertion, that if it were true, it could not be so much as made. The merely physical is transcended in every such assertion; and the man who has transcended it, rooted though his life be in nature, and one with the life of the whole and of all the past, must take the responsibility of living that life out on the high level of self-consciousness and morality which his very disclaimer involves. The sense of sin which wakes spontaneously with the perception that he is not what he ought to have been must not be explained away; at the level which life has reached in him, this is unscientific as well as immoral; his sin—for I do not know another word for it —must be realised as all that it is in the moral world if he is ever to be true to himself, not to say if he is ever to welcome the Atonement, and leave his sin behind. We have no need of words like sin and atonement—we could not have the experiences which they designate—unless we had a higher than merely natural life; and one of the tendencies of the modern mind which has to be counteracted by the evangelist is the tendency induced by physical and especially by biological science to explain the realities of personal experience by sub-personal categories. In conscience, in the sense of personal dignity, in the ultimate inability of man to deny the self which he is, we have always an appeal against such tendencies, which cannot fail; but it needs to be made resolutely when conscience is lethargic and the whole bias of the mind is to the other side.

Passing from physical science, the modern mind has perhaps been influenced most by the great idealist movement in philosophy—the movement which in Germany began with Kant and culminated in Hegel. This idealism, just like physical science, gives a certain stamp to the mind; when it takes possession of intelligence it casts it, so to speak, into a certain mould; even more than physical science it dominates it so that it becomes incapable of self-criticism, and very difficult to teach. Its importance to the preacher of Christianity is that it assumes certain relations between the human and the divine, relations which foreclose the very questions which the Atonement compels us to raise. To be brief, it teaches the essential unity of God and man. God and man, to speak of them as distinct, are necessary to each other, but man is as necessary to God as God is to man. God is the truth of man, but man is the reality of God. God comes to consciousness of Himself in man, and man in being conscious of himself is at the same time conscious of God. Though many writers of this school make a copious use of Christian phraseology, it seems to me obvious that it is not in an adequate Christian sense. Sin is not regarded as that which ought not to be, it is that which is to be transcended. It is as inevitable as anything in nature; and the sense of it, the bad conscience which accompanies it, is no more than the growing pains of the soul. On such a system there is no room for atonement in the sense of the mediation of God's forgiveness through Jesus Christ. We may consistently speak in it of a man being reconciled to himself, or even reconciled to his sins, but not, so far as I can understand, of his being reconciled to God, and still less, reconciled to God through the death of His Son. The penetration of Kant saw from the first all that could be made of atonement on the basis of any such system. What it means to the speculative mind is that the new man bears the sin of the old. When the sinner repents and is converted, the weight of what he has done comes home to him; the new man in him—the Son of God in him—accepts the responsibility of the old man, and so he has peace with God. Many whose minds are under the influence of this mode of thought do not see clearly to what it leads, and resent criticism of it as if it were a sort of impiety. Their philosophy is to them a surrogate for religion, but they should not be allowed to suppose (if they do suppose) that it is the equivalent of Christianity. There can be no Christianity without Christ; it is the presence of the Mediator which makes Christianity what it is. But a unique Christ, without Whom our religion disappears, is frankly disavowed by the more candid and outspoken of our idealist philosophers. Christ, they tell us, was certainly a man who had an early and a magnificently strong faith in the unity of the human and the Divine; but it was faith in a fact which enters into the constitution of every human consciousness, and it is absurd to suppose that the recognition of the fact, or the realisation of it, is essentially dependent on Him. He was not sinless—which is an expression without meaning, when we think of a human being which has to rise by conflict and self-suppression out of nature into the world of self-consciousness and right and wrong; He was not in any sense unique or exceptional; He was only what we all are in our degree; at best, He was only one among many great men who have contributed in their place and time to the spiritual elevation of the race. Such, I say, is the issue of this mode of thought as it is frankly avowed by some of its representative men; but the peculiarity of it, when it is obscurely fermenting as a leaven in the mind, is, that it appeals to men as having special affinities to Christianity. In our own country it is widely prevalent among those who have had a university education, and indeed in a much wider circle, and it is a serious question how we are to address our gospel to those who confront it in such a mental mood.

I have no wish to be unsympathetic, but I must frankly express my conviction that this philosophy only lives by ignoring the greatest reality of the spiritual world. There is something in that world—something with which we can come into intelligible and vital relations—something which can evince to our minds its truth and reality, for which this philosophy can make no room: Christ's consciousness of Himself. It is a theory of the universe which (on principle) cannot allow Christ to be anything else than an additional unit in the world's population; but if this were the truth about Him, no language could be strong enough to express the self-delusion in which He lived and died. That He was thus self-deluded is a hypothesis I do not feel called to discuss. One may be accused of subjectivity again, of course, though a subjective opinion which has the consent of the Christian centuries behind it need not tremble at hard names; but I venture to say that there is no reality in the world which more inevitably and uncompromisingly takes hold of the mind as a reality than our Lord's consciousness of Himself as it is attested to us in the Gospels. But when we have taken this reality for all that it is worth, the idealism just described is shaken to the foundation. What seemed to us so profound a truth —the essential unity of the human and the divine—may come to seem a formal and delusive platitude; in what we once regarded as the formula of the perfect religion—the divinity of man and the humanity of God—we may find quite as truly the formula of the first, not to say the final, sin. To see Christ not in the light of this speculative theorem, but in the light of His own consciousness of Himself, is to realise not only our kinship to God, but our remoteness from Him; it is to realise our incapacity for self-realisation when we are left to ourselves; it is to realise the need of the Mediator if we would come to the Father; it is to realise, in principle, the need of the Atonement, the need, and eventually the fact. When the modern mind therefore presents itself to us in this mood of philosophical competence, judging Christ from the point of view of the whole, and showing Him His place, we can only insist that the place is unequal to His greatness, and that His greatness cannot be explained away. The mind which is closed to the fact of His unique claims, and the unique relation to God on which they rest, is closed inevitably to the mediation of God's forgiveness through His death.

There is one other modification of mind, characteristic of modern times, of which we have yet to take account—I mean that which is produced by devotion to historical study. History is, as much as science, one of the achievements of our age; and the historical temper is as characteristic of the men we meet as the philosophical or the scientific. The historical temper, too, is just as apt as these others, perhaps unconsciously, perhaps quite consciously, but under the engaging plea of modesty, to pronounce absolute sentences which strike at the life of the Christian religion, and especially, therefore, at the idea of the Atonement. Sometimes this is done broadly, so that every one sees what it means. If we are told, for example, that everything historical is relative, that it belongs of necessity to a time, and is conditioned in ways so intricate that no knowledge can ever completely trace them; if we are told, further, that for this very reason nothing historical can have absolute significance, or can condition the eternal life of man, it is obvious that the Christian religion is being cut at the root. It is no use speaking about the Atonement—about the mediation of God's forgiveness to the soul through a historical person and work—if this is true. The only thing to be done is to raise the question whether it *is* true. It is no more for historical than for physical science to exalt itself into a theory of the universe, or to lay down the law with speculative absoluteness as to the significance and value which shall attach to facts. When we face the fact with which we are here concerned—the fact of Christ's consciousness of Himself and His vocation, to which reference has already been made—are we not forced to the conclusion that here a new spiritual magnitude has appeared in history, the very *differentia* of which is that it *has* eternal significance, and that it is eternal life to know it? If we are to preach the Atonement, we cannot allow either history or philosophy to proceed on assumptions which ignore or degrade the fact of Christ. Only a person in whom the eternal has become historical can be the bearer of the Atonement, and it must be our first concern to show, against all assumptions whether made in the name of history or of philosophy, that in point of fact there is such a person here.

This consideration requires to be kept in view even when we are dealing with the modern mind inside the Church. Nothing is commoner than to hear those who dissent from any given construction of the Atonement plead for a historical as opposed to a dogmatic interpretation of Christ. It is not always clear what is meant by this distinction, nor is it clear that those who use it are always conscious of what it would lead to if it were made absolute. Sometimes a dogmatic interpretation of the New Testament means an interpretation vitiated by dogmatic prejudice, an interpretation in which the meaning of the writers is missed because the mind is blinded by prepossessions of its own: in this sense a dogmatic interpretation is a thing which no one would defend. Sometimes, however, a dogmatic interpretation is one which reveals or discovers in the New Testament truths of eternal and divine significance, and to discredit such interpretation in the name of the historical is another matter. The distinction in this case, as has been already pointed out, is not absolute. It is analogous to the distinction between fact and theory, or between thing and meaning, or between efficient cause and final cause. None of these distinctions is absolute, and no intelligent mind would urge either side in them to the disparagement of the other. If we are to apprehend the whole reality presented to us, we must apprehend the theory as well as the fact, the meaning as well as the thing, the final as well as the efficient cause. In the subject with which we are dealing, this truth is frequently ignored. It is assumed, for example, that because Christ was put to death by His enemies, or because He died in the faithful discharge of His calling, therefore He did not die, in the sense of the Atonement, for our sins: the historical causes which brought about His death are supposed to preclude that interpretation of it according to which it mediates to us the divine forgiveness. But there is no incompatibility between the two things. To set aside an interpretation of Christ's death as dogmatic, on the ground that there is another which is historical, is like setting aside the idea that a watch is made to measure time because you know it was made by a watchmaker. It was both made by a watchmaker and made to measure time. Similarly it may be quite true both that Christ was crucified and slain by wicked men, and that He died for our sins. But without entering into the questions which this raises as to the relation between the wisdom of God and the course of human history, it is enough to be conscious of the prejudice which the historical temper is apt to generate against the recognition of the eternal in time. Surely it is a significant fact that the New Testament contains a whole series of books —the Johannine books—which have as their very burden the eternal significance of the historical: eternal life in Jesus Christ, come in flesh, the propitiation for the whole world. Surely also it is a significant fact of a different and even an ominous kind that we have at present in the Church a whole school of critics which is so far from appreciating the truth in this that it is hardly an exaggeration to say that it has devoted itself to a paltry and peddling criticism of these books in which the impression of the eternal is lost. But whether we are to be indebted to John's eyes, or to none but our own, if the eternal is not to be seen in Jesus, He can have no place in our religion; if the historical has no dogmatic content, it cannot be essential to eternal life. Hence if we believe and know that we have eternal life in Jesus, we must assert the truth which is implied in this against any conception of history which denies it. Nor is it really difficult to do so. With the experience of nineteen centuries behind us, we have only to confront this particular historical reality, Jesus Christ, without prejudice; in evangelising, we have only to confront others with Him; and we shall find it still possible to see God in Him, the Holy Father who through the Passion of His Son ministers to sinners the forgiveness of their sins.

In what has been said thus far by way of explaining the modern mind, emphasis may seem to have fallen mainly on those characteristics which make it less accessible than it might be to Christian truth, and especially to the Atonement. I have tried to point out the assailable side of its prepossessions, and to indicate the fundamental truths which must be asserted if our intellectual world is to be one in which the gospel may find room. But the modern mind has other characteristics. Some of these may have been exhibited hitherto mainly in criticising current representations of the Atonement; but in themselves they are entirely legitimate, and the claims they put forward are such as we cannot disown. Before proceeding to a further statement of the Atonement, I shall briefly refer to one or two of them: a doctrine of Atonement which did not satisfy them would undoubtedly stand condemned.

(1) The modern mind requires that everything shall be based on experience. Nothing is true or real to it which cannot be experimentally verified. This we shall all concede. But there is an inference sometimes drawn from it at which we may look with caution. It is the inference that, because everything must be based on experience, no appeal to Scripture has any authority. I have already explained in what sense it is possible to speak of the authority of Scripture, and here it is only necessary to make the simple remark that there is no proper

contrast between Scripture and experience. Scripture, so far as it concerns us here, is a record of experience or an interpretation of it. It was the Church's experience that it had its redemption in Christ; it was the interpretation of that experience that Christ died for our sins. Yet in emphasising experience the modern mind is right, and Scripture would lose its authority if the experience it describes were not perpetually verified anew.

(2) The modern mind desires to have everything in religion ethically construed. As a general principle this must command our unreserved assent. Anything which violates ethical standards, anything which is immoral or less than moral, must be excluded from religion. It may be, indeed, that ethical has sometimes been too narrowly defined. Ideas have been objected to as unethical which are really at variance not with a true perception of the constitution of humanity, and of the laws which regulate moral life, but with an atomic theory of personality under which moral life would be impossible. Persons are not atoms; in a sense they interpenetrate, though individuality has been called the true impenetrability. The world has been so constituted that we do not stand absolutely outside of each other; we can do things for each other. We can bear each other's burdens, and it is not unethical to say so, but the reverse. And again, it need not be unethical, though it transcends the ordinary sphere and range of ethical action, if we say that God in Christ is able to do for us what we cannot do for one another. With reference to the Atonement, the demand for ethical treatment is usually expressed in two ways. (*a*) There is the demand for analogies to it in human life. The demand is justifiable, in so far as God has made man in His own image; but, as has been suggested above, it has a limit, in so far as God is God and not man, and must have relations to the human race which its members do not and cannot have to each other. (*b*) There is the demand that the Atonement shall be exhibited in vital relation to a new life in which sin is overcome. This demand also is entirely legitimate, and it touches a weak point in the traditional Protestant doctrine. Dr. Chalmers tells us that he was brought up—such was the effect of the current orthodoxy upon him—in a certain distrust of good works. Some were certainly wanted, but not as being themselves salvation; only, as he puts it, as tokens of justification. It was a distinct stage in his religious progress when he realised that true justification sanctifies, and that the soul can and ought to abandon itself spontaneously and joyfully to do the good that it delights in. The modern mind assumes what Dr. Chalmers painfully discovered. An atonement that does not regenerate, it truly holds, is not an atonement in which men can be asked to believe. Such then, in its prejudices good and bad, is the mind to which the great truth of the Christian religion has to be presented.

[1] Of course this does not touch the fact that the whole 'authority' of the

Christian religion is in Jesus Himself—in His historical presence in the world, His words and works, His life and death and resurrection. He *is* the truth, the acceptance of which by man is life eternal.

CHAPTER II

We have now seen in a general way what is meant by the Atonement, and what are the characteristics of the mind to which the Atonement has to make its appeal. In that mind there is, as I believe, much which falls in with the Atonement, and prepares a welcome for it; but much also which creates prejudice against it, and makes it as possible still as in the first century to speak of the offence of the cross. No doubt the Atonement has sometimes been presented in forms which provoke antagonism, which challenge by an ostentation of unreason, or by a defiance of morality, the reason and conscience of man; but this alone does not explain the resentment which it often encounters. There is such a thing to be found in the world as the man who will have nothing to do with Christ on any terms, and who will least of all have anything to do with Him when Christ presents Himself in the character which makes man His debtor for ever. All men, as St. Paul says, have not faith: it is a melancholy fact, whether we can make anything of it or not. Discounting, however, this irrational or inexplicable opposition, which is not expressed in the mind but in the will, how are we to present the Atonement so that it shall excite the least prejudice, and find the most unimpeded access to the mind of our own generation? This is the question to which we have now to address ourselves.

To conceive the Atonement, that is, the fact that forgiveness is mediated to us through Christ, and specifically through His death, as clearly and truly as possible, it is necessary for us to realise the situation to which it is related. We cannot think of it except as related to a given situation. It is determined or conditioned by certain relations subsisting between God and man, as these relations have been affected by sin. What we must do, therefore, in the first instance, is to make clear to ourselves what these relations are, and how sin affects them.

To begin with, they are personal relations; they are relations the truth of which cannot be expressed except by the use of personal pronouns. We need not ask whether the personality of God can be proved antecedent to religion, or as a basis for a religion yet to be established; in the only sense in which we can be concerned with it, religion is an experience of the personality of God, and of our own personality in relation to it. 'O Lord, *Thou* hast searched *me* and known *me*.' '*I* am continually with *Thee*! No human experience can be more vital or more normal than that which is expressed in these words, and no argument, be it ever so subtle or so baffling, can weigh a feather's-weight against such experience. The same conception of the relations of God and man is expressed again as unmistakably in every word of Jesus about the Father and the Son and the nature of their communion with each other. It is only in such personal relations that the kind of situation can emerge, and the kind of experience be had, with which the Atonement deals; and antecedent to such experience, or in independence of it, the Atonement must remain an incredible because an unrealisable thing.

But to say that the relations of God and man are personal is not enough. They are not only personal, but universal. *Personal* is habitually used in a certain contrast with *legal*, and it is very easy to lapse into the idea that personal relations, because distinct from legal ones, are independent of law; but to say the least of it, that is an ambiguous and misleading way of describing the facts. The relations of God and man are not lawless, they are not capricious, incalculable, incapable of moral meaning; they are personal, but determined by something of universal import; in other words, they are not merely personal but ethical. That is ethical which is at once personal and universal. Perhaps the simplest way to make this evident is to notice that the relations of man to God are the relations to God not of atoms, or of self-contained individuals, each of which is a world in itself, but of individuals which are essentially related to each other, and bound up in the unity of a race. The relations of God to man, therefore, are not capricious though they are personal: they are reflected or expressed in a moral constitution to which all personal beings are equally bound, a moral constitution of eternal and universal validity, which neither God nor man can ultimately treat as anything else than what it is.

This is a point at which some prejudice has been raised against the Atonement by theologians, and more, perhaps, by persons protesting against what they supposed theologians to mean. If one may be excused a personal reference, few things have astonished me more than to be charged with teaching a 'forensic' or 'legal' or 'judicial' doctrine of Atonement, resting, as such a doctrine must do, on a 'forensic' or 'legal' or 'judicial' conception of man's relation to God. It is all the more astonishing when the charge is combined with what one can only decline as in the circumstances totally unmerited compliments to the clearness with which he has expressed himself. There is nothing which I should wish to reprobate more whole-heartedly than the conception which is expressed by these words. To say that the relations of God and man are forensic is to say that they are regulated by statute—that sin is a breach of statute—that the sinner is a criminal—and that God adjudicates on him by interpreting the statute in its application to his case. Everybody knows that this is a travesty of the truth, and it is surprising that any one should be charged with teaching it, or that any one should applaud himself, as though he were in the foremost files of time, for not believing it. It is superfluously apparent that the relations of God and man are not those of a magistrate on the bench pronouncing according to the act on the criminal at the bar. To say this, however, does not make these relations more intelligible. In particular, to say that they are personal, as opposed to forensic, does not make them more intelligible. If they are to be rational, if they are to be moral, if they are to be relations in which an ethical life can be lived, and ethical responsibilities realised, they must be not only personal, but universal; they must be relations that in some sense are determined by law. Even to say that they are the relations, not of judge and criminal, but of Father and child, does not get us past this point. The relations of father and child are undoubtedly more adequate to the truth than those of judge and criminal; they are more adequate, but so far as our experience of them goes, they are not equal to it. If the sinner is not a criminal before his judge, neither is he a naughty child before a parent whose own weakness or affinity to evil introduces an incalculable element into his dealing with his child's fault. I should not think of saying that it is the desire to escape from the inexorableness of law to a God capable of indulgent human tenderness that inspires the violent protests so often heard against 'forensic' and 'legal' ideas: but that is the impression which one sometimes involuntarily receives from them. It ought to be apparent to every one that even the relation of parent and child, if it is to be a moral relation, must be determined in a way which has universal and final validity. It must be a relation in which—ethically speaking—some things are for ever obligatory, and some things for ever impossible; in other words, it must be a relation determined by law, and law which cannot deny itself. But law in this sense is not 'legal.' It is not 'judicial,' or 'forensic,' or 'statutory.' None the less it is real and vital, and the whole moral value of the relation depends upon it. When a man says—as some one has said—'There are many to whom the conception of forgiveness resting on a judicial transaction does not appeal at all,' I entirely agree with him; it does not appeal at all to me. But what would be the value of a forgiveness which did not recognise in its eternal truth and worth that universal law in which the relations of God and man are constituted? Without the recognition of that law—that moral order or constitution in which we have our life in relation to God and each other— righteousness and sin, atonement and forgiveness, would all alike be words without meaning.

In connection with this, reference may be made to an important point in the interpretation of the New Testament. The responsibility for what is called the forensic conception of the Atonement is often traced to St. Paul, and the greatest of all the ministers of grace is not infrequently spoken of as though he had deliberately laid the most insuperable of stumbling-blocks in the way to the gospel. Most people, of course, are conscious that they do not look well talking down to St. Paul, and occasionally one can detect a note of misgiving in the brave words in which his doctrine is renounced, a note of misgiving which suggests that the charitable course is to hear such protests in silence, and to let those who utter them think over the matter again. But there is what claims to be a scientific way of expressing dissent from the apostle, a way which, equally with the petulant one, rests, I am convinced, on misapprehension of his teaching. This it would not be fair to ignore. It interprets what the apostle says about law solely by reference to the great question at issue between the Jewish and the Christian religions, making the word law mean the statutory system under which the Jews lived, and nothing else. No one will deny that Paul does use the word in this sense; the law often means for him specifically the law of Moses. The law of Moses, however, never means for him anything less than the law of God; it is one specific form in which the universal relations subsisting between God and man, and making religion and morality possible, have found historical expression. But Paul's mind does not rest in this one historical expression. He generalises it. He has the conception of a universal law, to which he can appeal in Gentile as well as in Jew—a law in the presence of which sin is revealed, and by the reaction of which sin is judged—a law which God could not deny without denying Himself, and to which justice is done (in other words, which is maintained in its integrity), even when God justifies the ungodly. But when law is thus universalised, it ceases to be legal; it is not a statute, but the moral constitution of the world. Paul preached the same gospel to the Gentiles as he did to the Jews; he preached in it the same relation of the Atonement and of Christ's death to divine law. But he did not do this by extending to all mankind a Pharisaic, legal, forensic relation to God: he did it by rising above such conceptions, even though as a Pharisee he may have had to start from them, to the conception of a relation of all men to God expressing itself in a moral constitution—or, as he would have said, but in an entirely unforensic sense, in a law—of divine and unchanging validity. The maintenance of this law, or of this moral constitution, in its inviolable integrity was the signature of the forgiveness Paul preached. The Atonement meant to him that forgiveness was mediated through One in whose life and death the most signal homage was paid to this law: the very glory of the Atonement was that it manifested the righteousness of God; it demonstrated God's consistency with His own character, which would have been violated alike by indifference to sinners and by indifference to that universal moral order—that law of God —in which alone eternal life is possible.

Hence it is a mistake to say—though this also has been said—that 'Paul's problem was not that of the possibility of forgiveness; it was the Jewish law, the Old Testament dispensation: how to justify his breach with it, how to demonstrate that the old order had been annulled and a new order inaugurated.' There is a false contrast in all such propositions. Paul's problem was that of the Jewish law, and it was also that of the possibility of forgiveness; it was that of the Jewish law, and it was also that of a revelation of grace, in which God should justify the ungodly, Jew or Gentile, and yet maintain inviolate those universal moral relations between Himself and man for which law is the compendious expression. It does not matter whether we suppose him to start from the concrete instance of the Jewish law, and to generalise on the basis of it; or to start from the universal conception of law, and to recognise in existing Jewish institutions the most available and definite illustration of it: in either case, the only Paul whose mind is known to us has completely transcended the forensic point of view. The same false contrast is repeated when we are told that, 'That doctrine (Paul's "juristic doctrine") had its origin, not so much in his religious experience, as in apologetic necessities.' The only apologetic necessities which give rise to fundamental doctrines are those created by religious experience. The apologetic of any religious experience is just the definition of it as real in relation to other acknowledged realities. Paul had undoubtedly an apologetic of forgiveness— namely, his doctrine of atonement. But the acknowledged reality in relation to which he defined forgiveness—the reality with which, by means of his doctrine of atonement, he showed forgiveness to be consistent—was not the law of the Jews (though that was included in it, or might be pointed to in illustration of it): it was the law of God, the universal and inviolable order in which alone eternal life is possible, and in which all men, and not the Jews only, live and move and have their being. It was the perception of this which made Paul an apostle to the Gentiles, and it is this very thing itself, which some would degrade into an awkward, unintelligent, and outworn rag of Pharisaic apologetic, which is the very heart and soul of Paul's Gentile gospel. Paul himself was perfectly conscious of this; he could not have preached to the Gentiles at all unless he had been. But there is nothing in it which can be characterised as 'legal,' 'judicial,' or 'forensic'; and of this also, I have no doubt, the apostle was well aware. Of course he occupied a certain historical position, had certain historical questions to answer, was subject to historical limitations of different kinds; but I have not the courage to treat him, nor do his words entitle any one to do so, as a man who in the region of ideas could not put two and two together.

But to return to the point from which this digression on St. Paul started. We have seen that the relations of God and man are personal, and also that they are universal, that is, there is a law of them, or, if we like to say so, a law in them, on the maintenance of which their whole ethical value depends. The next point to be noticed is that these relations are deranged or disordered by sin. Sin is, in fact, nothing else than this derangement or disturbance: it is that in which wrong is done to the moral constitution under which we live. And let no one say that in such an expression we are turning our back on the personal world, and lapsing, or incurring the risk of lapsing, into mere legalism again. It cannot be too often repeated that if the universal element, or law, be eliminated from personal relations, there is nothing intelligible left: no reason, no morality, no religion, no sin or righteousness or forgiveness, nothing to appeal to mind or conscience. In the widest sense of the word, sin, as a disturbance of the personal relations between God and man, is a violence done to the constitution under which God and man form one moral community, share, as we may reverently express it, one life, have in view the same moral ends.

It is no more necessary in connection with the Atonement than in any other connection that we should have a doctrine of the origin of sin. We do not know its origin, we only know that it is here. We cannot observe the genesis of the bad conscience any more than we can observe the genesis of consciousness in general. We see that consciousness does stand in relief against the background of natural life; but though we believe that, as it exists in us, it has emerged from that background, we cannot see it emerge; it is an ultimate fact, and is assumed in all that we can ever regard as its physical antecedents and presuppositions. In the same way, the moral consciousness is an ultimate fact, and irreducible. The physical theory of evolution must not be allowed to mislead us here, and in particular it must not be allowed to discredit the conception of moral responsibility for sin which is embodied in the story of the Fall. Each of us individually has risen into moral life from a mode of being which was purely natural; in other words, each of us, individually, has been a subject of evolution; but each of us also has fallen— fallen, presumably, in ways determined by his natural constitution, yet certainly, as conscience assures us, in ways for which we are morally answerable, and to which, in the moral constitution of the world, consequences attach which we must recognise as our due. They are not only results of our action, but results which that action has merited, and there is no moral hope for us unless we accept them as such. Now what is true of any, or rather of all, of us, without compromise of the moral consciousness, may be true of the race, or of the first man, if there was a first man. Evolution and a Fall cannot be inconsistent, for both enter into every moral experience of which we know anything; and no opinion we hold about the origin of sin can make it anything else than it is in conscience, or give its results any character other than that which they have to conscience. Of course when one tries to interpret sin outside of conscience, as though it were purely physical, and did not have its being in personality, consciousness, and will, it disappears; and the laborious sophistries of such interpretations must be left to themselves. The point for us is that no matter how sin originated, in the moral consciousness in which it has its being it is recognised as a derangement of the vital relations of man, a violation of that universal order outside of which he has no true good.

In what way, now, let us ask, does the reality of sin come home to the sinner? How does he recognise it as what it is? What is the reaction against the sinner, in the moral order under which he lives, which reveals to him the meaning of his sinful act or state?

In the first place, there is that instantaneous but abiding reaction which is called the bad conscience—the sense of guilt, of being answerable to God for sin. The sin may be an act which is committed in a moment, but in this aspect of it, at least, it does not fade into the past. An animal may have a past, for anything we can tell, and naturalistic interpreters of sin may believe that sin dies a natural death with time, and need not trouble us permanently; but this is not the voice of conscience, in which alone sin exists, and which alone can tell us the truth about it. The truth is that the spiritual being has no past. Just as he is continually with God, his sin is continually with him. He cannot escape it by not thinking. When he keeps silence, as the Psalmist says—and that is always his first resource, as though, if he were to say nothing about it, God might say nothing about it, and the whole thing blow over—it devours him like a fever within: his bones wax old with his moaning all day long. This sense of being wrong with God, under His displeasure, excluded from His fellowship, afraid to meet Him yet bound to meet Him, is the sense of guilt. Conscience confesses in it its liability to God, a liability which in the very nature of the case it can do nothing to meet, and which therefore is nearly akin to despair.

But the bad conscience, real as it is, may be too abstractly interpreted. Man is not a pure spirit, but a spiritual being whose roots strike to the very depths of nature, and who is connected by the most intimate and vital relations not only with his fellow-creatures of the same species, but with the whole system of nature in which he lives. The moral constitution in which he has his being comprehends, if we may say so, nature in itself: the God who has established the moral order in which man lives, has established the natural order also as part of the same whole with it. In some profound way the two are one. We distinguish in man, legitimately enough, between the spiritual and the physical; but man is one, and the universe in which he lives is one, and in man's relation to God the distinction of physical and spiritual must ultimately disappear. The sin which introduces disorder into man's relations to God produces reactions affecting man as a whole—not reactions that, as we sometimes say, are purely spiritual, but reactions as broad as man's being and as the whole divinely constituted environment in which it lives. I am well aware of the difficulty of giving expression to this truth, and of the hopelessness of trying to give expression to it by means of those very distinctions which it is its nature to transcend. The distinctions are easy and obvious; what we have to learn is that they are not final. It seems so conclusive to say, as some one has done in criticising the idea of atonement, that spiritual transgressing brings spiritual penalty, and physical brings physical; it seems so conclusive, and it is in truth so completely beside the mark. We cannot divide either man or the universe in this fashion into two parts which move on different planes and have no vital relations; we cannot, to apply this truth to the subject before us, limit the divine reaction against sin, or the experiences through which, in any case whatever, sin is brought home to man as what it is, to the purely spiritual sphere. Every sin is a sin of the indivisible human being, and the divine reaction against it expresses itself to conscience through the indivisible frame of that world, at once natural and spiritual, in which man lives. We cannot distribute evils into the two classes of physical and moral, and subsequently investigate the relation between them: if we could, it would be of no service here. What we have to understand is that when a man sins he does something in which his whole being participates, and that the reaction of God against his sin is a reaction in which he is conscious, or might be conscious, that the whole system of things is in arms against him.

There are those, no doubt, to whom this will seem fantastic, but it is a truth, I am convinced, which is presupposed in the Christian doctrine of Atonement, as the mediation of forgiveness through the suffering and death of Christ: and it is a truth also, if I am not much mistaken, to which all the highest poetry, which is also the deepest vision of the human mind, bears witness. We may distinguish natural law and moral law as sharply as we please, and it is as necessary sometimes as it is easy to make these sharp and absolute distinctions; but there is a unity in experience which makes itself felt deeper than all the antitheses of logic, and in that unity nature and spirit are no more defined by contrast with each other: on the contrary, they interpenetrate and support each other: they are aspects of the same whole. When we read in the prophet Amos, 'Lo, He that formeth the mountains, and createth the wind, and declareth unto man what is his thought, that maketh the morning darkness and treadeth upon the high places of the earth, the Lord, the God of hosts, is His name,' this is the truth which is expressed. The power which reveals itself in conscience—telling us all things that ever we did, declaring unto us what is our thought—is the same which reveals itself in nature, establishing the everlasting hills, creating the winds which sweep over them, turning the shadow of death into the morning and making the day dark with night, calling for the waters of the sea, and pouring them out on the face of the earth. Conscience speaks in a still small voice, but it is no impotent voice; it can summon the thunder to give it resonance; the power which we sometimes speak of as if it were purely spiritual is a power which clothes itself spontaneously and of right in all the majesty and omnipotence of nature. It is the same truth, again, in another aspect of it, which is expressed in Wordsworth's sublime lines to Duty:

'Thou dost preserve the Stars from wrong,
And the most ancient Heavens through Thee are fresh and strong.'

When the mind sees deepest, it is conscious that it needs more than physical astronomy, more than spectrum analysis, to tell us everything even about the stars. There is a moral constitution, it assures us, even of the physical world; and though it is impossible for us to work it out in detail, the assumption of it is the only assumption on which we can understand the life of a being related as man is related both to the natural and the spiritual. I do not pretend to prove that there is articulate or conscious reflection on this in either the Old Testament or the New; I take it for granted, as self-evident, that this sense of the ultimate unity of the natural and the spiritual—which is, indeed, but one form of belief in God—pervades the Bible from beginning to end. It knows nothing of our abstract and absolute distinctions; to come to the matter in hand, it knows nothing of a sin which has merely spiritual penalties. Sin is the act or the state of man, and the reaction against it is the reaction of the whole order, at once natural and spiritual, in which man lives.

Now the great difficulty which the modern mind has with the Atonement, or with the representation of it in the New Testament, is that it assumes some kind of connection between sin and death. Forgiveness is mediated through Christ, but specifically through His death. He died for our sins; if we can be put right with God apart from this, then, St. Paul tells us, He died for nothing. One is almost ashamed to repeat that this is not Paulinism, but the Christianity of the whole Apostolic Church. What St. Paul made the basis of his preaching, that Christ died for our sins, according to the Scriptures, he had on his own showing received as the common Christian tradition. But is there anything in it? Can we receive it simply on the authority of the primitive Church? Can we realise any such connection between death and sin as makes it a truth to us, an intelligible, impressive, overpowering thought, that Christ died for our sins?

I venture to say that a great part of the difficulty which is felt at this point is due to the false abstraction just referred to. Sin is put into one world—the moral; death is put into another world—the natural; and there is no connection between them. This is very convincing if we find it possible to believe that we live in two unconnected worlds. But if we find it impossible to believe this—and surely the impossibility is patent—its plausibility is gone. It is a shining example of this false abstraction when we are told, as though it were a conclusive objection to all that the New Testament has to say about the relation of sin and death, that 'the specific penalty of sin is not a fact of the natural life, but of the moral life.' What right has any one, in speaking of the ultimate realities in human life, of those experiences in which man becomes conscious of all that is involved in his relations to God and their disturbance by sin, to split that human life into 'natural' and 'moral,' and fix an impassable gulf between? The distinction is legitimate, as has already been remarked, within limits, but it is not final; and what the New Testament teaches, or rather assumes, about the relation of sin and death, is one of the ways in which we are made sensible that it is not final. Sin and death do not belong to unrelated worlds. As far as man is concerned, the two worlds, to use an inadequate figure, intersect; and at one point in the line of their intersection sin and death meet and interpenetrate. In the indivisible experience of man he is conscious that they are parts or aspects of the same thing.

That this is what Scripture means when it assumes the connection of death and sin is not to be refuted by pointing either to the third chapter of Genesis or to the fifth of Romans. It does not, for example, do justice either to Genesis or to St. Paul to say, as has been said, that according to their representation, 'Death—not spiritual, but natural death—is the direct consequence of sin and its specific penalty.' In such a dictum, the distinctions again mislead. To read the third chapter of Genesis in this sense would mean that what we had to find in it was a mythological explanation of the origin of physical death. But does any one believe that any Bible writer was ever curious about this question? or does any one believe that a mythological solution of the problem, how death originated—a solution which *ex hypothesi* has not a particle of truth or even of meaning in it—could have furnished the presupposition for the fundamental doctrine of the Christian religion, that Christ died for our sins, and that in Him we have our forgiveness through His blood? A truth which has appealed so powerfully to man cannot be sustained on a falsehood. That the third chapter of Genesis is mythological in form, no one who knows what mythology is will deny; but even mythology is not made out of nothing, and in this chapter every atom is 'stuff o' the conscience.' What we see in it is conscience, projecting as it were in a picture on a screen its own invincible, dear-bought, despairing conviction that sin and death are indissolubly united —that from death the sinful race can never get away—that it is part of the indivisible reality of sin that the shadow of death darkens the path of the sinner, and at last swallows him up. It is this also which is in the mind of St. Paul when he says that by one man sin entered into the world and death by sin. It is not the origin of death he is interested in, nor the origin of sin either, but the fact that sin and death hang together. And just because sin is sin, this is not a fact of natural history, or a fact which natural history can discredit. Scripture has no interest in natural history, nor does such an interest help us to understand it. It is no doubt perfectly true that to the biologist death is part of the indispensable machinery of nature; it is a piece of the mechanism without which the movement of the whole would be arrested; to put it so, death to the biologist is part of the same whole as life, or life and death are for him aspects of one thing. One can admit this frankly without compromising, because without touching, the other and deeper truth which is so interesting and indeed so vital alike in the opening pages of revelation and in its consummation in the Atonement. The biologist, when he deals with man, and with his life and death, deliberately deals with them in abstraction, as merely physical phenomena; to him man is a piece of nature, and he is nothing more. But the Biblical writers deal with man in the integrity of his being, and in his relations to God; they transcend the distinction of natural and moral, because for God it is not final: they are sensible of the unity in things which the everyday mind, for practical purposes, finds it convenient to keep apart. It is one great instance of this that they are sensible of the unity of sin and death. We may call sin a spiritual thing, but the man who has never felt the shadow of death fall upon it does not know what that spiritual thing is: and we may call death a natural thing, but the man who has not felt its natural pathos deepen into tragedy as he faced it with the sense of sin upon him does not know what that natural thing is. We are here, in short, at the vanishing point of this distinction—God is present, and nature and spirit interpenetrate in His presence. We hear much in other connections of the sacramental principle, and its importance for the religious interpretation of nature. It is a sombre illustration of this principle if we say that death is a kind of sacrament of sin. It is in death, ultimately, that the whole meaning of sin comes home to the sinner; he has not sounded it to its depths till he has discovered that this comes into it at last. And we must not suppose that when Paul read the third chapter of Genesis he read it as a mythological explanation of the origin of physical death, and accepted it as such on the authority of inspiration. With all his reverence for the Old Testament, Paul accepted nothing from it that did not speak to his conscience, and waken echoes there; and what so spoke to him from the third chapter of Genesis was not a mythical story of how death invaded Paradise, but the profound experience of the human race expressed in the story, an experience in which sin and death inter-penetrate, interpret, and in a sense constitute each other. To us they are what they are only in relation to each other, and when we deny the relation we see the reality of neither. This is the truth, as I apprehend it, of all we are taught either in the Old Testament or in the New about the relation of sin and death. It is part of the greater truth that what we call the physical and spiritual worlds are ultimately one, being constituted with a view to each other; and most of the objections which are raised against it are special cases of the objections which are raised against the recognition of this ultimate unity. So far as they are such, it is not necessary to discuss them further; and so far as the ultimate unity of the natural and the spiritual is a truth rather to be experienced than demonstrated, it is not probable that much can be done by argument to gain acceptance for the idea that sin and death have essential relations to each other. But there are particular objections to this idea to which it may be worth while to refer.

There is, to begin with, the undoubted fact that many people live and die without, consciously at least, recognising this relation. The thought of death may have had a very small place in their lives, and when death itself comes it may, for various reasons, be a very insignificant experience to them. It may come in a moment, suddenly, and give no time for feeling; or it may come as the last step in a natural process of decay, and arrest life almost unconsciously; or it may come through a weakness in which the mind wanders to familiar scenes of the past, living these over again, and in a manner escaping by so doing the awful experience of death itself; or it may come in childhood before the moral consciousness is fully awakened, and moral reflection and experience possible. This last case, properly speaking, does not concern us; we do not know how to define sin in relation to those in whom the moral consciousness is as yet undeveloped: we only know that somehow or other they are involved in the moral as well as in the natural unity of the race. But leaving them out of account, is there any real difficulty in the others? any real objection to the Biblical idea that sin and death in humanity are essentially related? I do not think there is. To say that many people are unconscious of the connection is only another way of saying that many people fail to realise in full and tragic reality what is meant by death and sin. They think very little about either. The third chapter of Genesis could never have been written out of their conscience. Sin is not for them all one with despair: they are not, through fear of death, all their lifetime subject to bondage. Scripture, of course, has no difficulty in admitting this; it depicts, on the amplest scale, and in the most vivid colours, the very kind of life and death which are here supposed. But it does not consider that such a life and death are *ipso facto* a refutation of the truth it teaches about the essential relations of death and sin. On the contrary, it considers them a striking demonstration of that moral dulness and insensibility in man which must be overcome if he is ever to see and feel his sin as what it is to God, or welcome the Atonement as that in which God's forgiveness of sin is mediated through the tremendous experience of death. I know there are those who will call this arrogant, or even insolent, as though I were passing a moral sentence on all who do not accept a theorem of mine; but I hope I do not need here to disclaim any such unchristian temper. Only, it is necessary to insist that the connection of sin and death in Scripture is neither a fantastic piece of mythology, explaining, as mythology does, the origin of a physical law, nor, on the other hand, a piece of supernaturally revealed history, to be accepted on the authority of Him who has revealed it; in such revelations no one believes any longer; it is a profound conviction and experience of the human conscience, and all that is of interest is to show that such a conviction and experience can never be set aside by the protest of those who aver that they know nothing about it. One must insist on this, however it may expose him to the charge of judging. Can we utter any truth at all, in which conscience is concerned, and which is not universally acknowledged, without seeming to judge?

Sometimes, apart from the general denial of any connection between death and sin, it is pointed out that death has another and a totally different character. Death in any given case may be so far from coming as a judgment of God, that it actually comes as a gracious gift from Him; it may even be an answer to prayer, a merciful deliverance from pain, an event welcomed by suffering human nature, and by all who sympathise with it. This is quite true, but again, one must point out, rests on the false abstraction so often referred to. Man is regarded in all this simply in the character of a sufferer, and death as that which brings suffering to an end; but that is not all the truth about man, nor all the truth about death. Physical pain may be so terrible that consciousness is absorbed and exhausted in it, sometimes even extinguished, but it is not to such abnormal conditions we should appeal to discover the deepest truths in the moral consciousness of man. If the waves of pain subsided, and the whole nature collected its forces again, and conscience was once more audible, death too would be seen in a different light. It might not indeed be apprehended at once, as Scripture apprehends it, but it would not be regarded simply as a welcome relief from pain. It would become possible to see in it something through which God spoke to the conscience, and eventually to realise its intimate relation to sin.

The objections we have just considered are not very serious, because they practically mean that death has no moral character at all; they reduce it to a natural phenomenon, and do not bring it into any relation to the conscience. It is a more respectable, and perhaps a more formidable objection, when death is brought into the moral world, and when the plea is put forward that so far from being God's judgment upon sin, it may be itself a high moral achievement. A man may die greatly; his death may be a triumph; nothing in his life may become him like the leaving it. Is not this inconsistent with the idea that there is any peculiar connection between death and sin? From the Biblical point of view the answer must again be in the negative. There is no such triumph over death as makes death itself a noble ethical achievement, which is not at the same time a triumph over sin. Man vanquishes the one only as in the grace of God he is able to vanquish the other. The doom that is in death passes away only as the sin to which it is related is transcended. But there is more than this to be said. Death cannot be so completely an action that it ceases to be a passion; it cannot be so completely achieved that it ceases to be accepted or endured. And in this last aspect of it the original character which it bore in relation to sin still makes itself felt. Transfigure it, as it may be transfigured, by courage, by devotion, by voluntary abandonment of life for a higher good, and it remains nevertheless the last enemy. There is something in it monstrous and alien to the spirit, something which baffles the moral intelligence, till the truth dawns upon us that for all our race sin and death are aspects of one thing. If we separate them, we understand neither; nor do we understand the solemn greatness of martyrdom itself if we regard it as a triumph only, and eliminate from the death which martyrs die all sense of the universal relation in humanity of death and sin. No one knew the spirit of the martyr more thoroughly than St. Paul. No one could speak more confidently and triumphantly of death than he. No one knew better how to turn the passion into action, the endurance into a great spiritual achievement. But also, no one knew better than he, in consistency with all this, that sin and death are needed for the interpretation of each other, and that fundamentally, in the experience of the race, they constitute one whole. Even when he cried, 'O death, where is thy sting?' he was conscious that 'the sting of death is sin.' Each, so to speak, had its reality in the other. No one could vanquish death who had not vanquished sin. No one could know what sin meant without tasting death. These were not mythological fancies in St. Paul's mind, but the conviction in which the Christian conscience experimentally lived, and moved, and had its being. And these convictions, I repeat, furnish the point of view from which we must appreciate the Atonement, *i.e.* the truth that forgiveness, as Christianity preaches it, is specifically mediated through Christ's death.

CHAPTER III

What has now been said about the relations subsisting between God and man, about the manner in which these relations are affected by sin, and particularly about the Scripture doctrine of the connection between sin and death, must determine, to a great extent, our attitude to the Atonement. The Atonement, as the New Testament presents it, assumes the connection of sin and death. Apart from some sense and recognition of such connection, the mediation of forgiveness through the death of Christ can only appear an arbitrary, irrational, unacceptable idea. But leaving the Atonement meanwhile out of sight, and looking only at the situation created by sin, the question inevitably arises, What can be done with it? Is it possible to remedy or to reverse it? It is an abnormal and unnatural situation; can it be annulled, and the relations of God and man put upon an ideal footing? Can God forgive sin and restore the soul? Can we claim that He shall? And if it is possible for Him to do so, can we tell how or on what conditions it is possible?

When the human mind is left to itself, there are only two answers which it can give to these questions. Perhaps they are not specially characteristic of the modern mind, but the modern mind in various moods has given passionate expression to both of them. The first says roundly that forgiveness is impossible. Sin is, and it abides. The sinner can never escape from the past. His future is mortgaged to it, and it cannot be redeemed. He can never get back the years which the locust has eaten. His leprous flesh can never come again like the flesh of a little child. Whatsoever a man soweth, that shall he also reap, and reap for ever and ever. It is not eternal punishment which is incredible; nothing else has credibility. Let there be no illusion about this: forgiveness is a violation, a reversal, of law, and no such thing is conceivable in a world in which law reigns.

The answer to this is, that sin and its consequences are here conceived as though they belonged to a purely physical world, whereas, if the world were only physical, there could be no such thing as sin. As soon as we realise that sin belongs to a world in which freedom is real—a world in which reality means the personal relations subsisting between man and God, and the experiences realised in these relations—the question assumes a different aspect. It is not one of logic or of physical law, but of personality, of character, of freedom. There is at least a possibility that the sinner's relation to his sin and God's relation to the sinner should change, and that out of these changed relations a regenerative power should spring, making the sinner, after all, a new creature. The question, of course, is not decided in this sense, but it is not foreclosed.

At the opposite extreme from those who pronounce forgiveness impossible stand those who give the second answer to the great question, and calmly assure us that forgiveness may be taken for granted. They emphasise what the others overlooked—the personal character of the relations of God and man. God is a loving Father; man is His weak and unhappy child; and of course God forgives. As Heine put it, *c'est mon métier*, it is what He is for. But the conscience which is really burdened by sin does not easily find satisfaction in this cheap pardon. There is something in conscience which will not allow it to believe that God can simply condone sin: to take forgiveness for granted, when you realise what you are doing, seems to a live conscience impious and profane. In reality, the tendency to take forgiveness for granted is the tendency of those who, while they properly emphasise the personal character of the relations of God and man, overlook their universal character—that is, exclude from them that element of law without which personal relations cease to be ethical. But a forgiveness which ignores this stands in no relation to the needs of the soul or the character of God.

What the Christian religion holds to be the truth about forgiveness—a truth embodied in the Atonement—is something quite distinct from both the propositions which have just been considered. The New Testament does not teach, with the naturalistic or the legal mind, that forgiveness is impossible; neither does it teach, with the sentimental or lawless mind, that it may be taken for granted. It teaches that forgiveness is mediated to sinners through Christ, and specifically through His death: in other words, that it is possible for God to forgive, but possible for God only through a supreme revelation of His love, made at infinite cost, and doing justice to the uttermost to those inviolable relations in which alone, as I have already said, man can participate in eternal life, the life of God Himself—doing justice to them as relations in which there is an inexorable divine reaction against sin, finally expressing itself in death. It is possible on these terms, and it becomes actual as sinful men open their hearts in penitence and faith to this marvellous revelation, and abandon their sinful life unreservedly to the love of God in Christ who died for them.

From this point of view it seems to me possible to present in a convincing and persuasive light some of the truths involved in the Atonement to which the modern mind is supposed to be specially averse.

Thus it becomes credible—we say so not *à priori*, but after experience—that there is a *divine necessity* for it; in other words, there is no forgiveness possible to God without it: if He forgives at all, it must be in this way and in no other. To say so beforehand would be inconceivably presumptuous, but it is quite another thing to say so after the event. What it really means is that in the very act of forgiving sin—or, to use the daring word of St. Paul, in the very act of justifying the ungodly—God must act in consistency with His whole character. He must demonstrate Himself to be what He is in relation to sin, a God with whom evil cannot dwell, a God who maintains inviolate the moral constitution of the world, taking sin as all that it is in the very process through which He mediates His forgiveness to men.

It is the recognition of this divine necessity—not to forgive, but to forgive in a way which shows that God is irreconcilable to evil, and can never treat it as other or less than it is—it is the recognition of this divine necessity, or the failure to recognise it, which ultimately divides interpreters of Christianity into evangelical and non-evangelical, those who are true to the New Testament and those who cannot digest it.

No doubt the forms in which this truth is expressed are not always adequate to the idea they are meant to convey, and if we are only acquainted with them at second hand they will probably appear even less adequate than they are. When Athanasius, *e.g.*, speaks of God's *truth* in this connection, and then reduces God's truth to the idea that God must keep His word—the word which made death the penalty of sin—we may feel that the form only too easily loses contact with the substance. Yet Athanasius is dealing with the essential fact of the case, that God must be true to Himself, and to the moral order in which men live, in all His dealings with sin for man's deliverance from it; and that He has been thus true to Himself in sending His Son to live our life and to die our death for our salvation. Or again, when Anselm in the *Cur Deus Homo* speaks of the satisfaction which is rendered to God for the infringement of His honour by sin—a satisfaction apart from which there can be no forgiveness—we may feel again, and even more strongly, that the form of the thought is inadequate to the substance. But what Anselm means is that sin makes a real difference to God, and that even in forgiving God treats that difference *as* real, and cannot do otherwise. He cannot ignore it, or regard it as other or less than it is; if He did so, He would not be more gracious than He is in the Atonement, He would cease to be God. It is Anselm's profound grasp of this truth which, in spite of all its inadequacy in form, and of all the criticism to which its inadequacy has exposed it, makes the *Cur Deus Homo* the truest and greatest book on the Atonement that has ever been written. It is the same truth of a divine necessity for the Atonement which is emphasised by St. Paul in the third chapter of Romans, where he speaks of Christ's death as a demonstration of God's righteousness. Christ's death, we may paraphrase his meaning, is an act in which (so far as it is ordered in God's providence)

God does justice to Himself. He does justice to His character as a gracious God, undoubtedly, who is moved with compassion for sinners: if He did not act in a way which displayed His compassion for sinners, He would *not* do justice to Himself; there would be no [Greek] *endeixis* of His [Greek] *dikaiosune*: it would be in abeyance: He would do Himself an injustice, or be untrue to Himself. It is with this in view that we can appreciate the arguments of writers like Diestel and Ritschl, that God's righteousness is synonymous with His grace. Such arguments are true to this extent, that God's righteousness includes His grace. He could not demonstrate it, He could not be true to Himself, if His grace remained hidden. We must not, however, conceive of this as if it constituted on our side a claim upon grace or upon forgiveness: such a claim would be a contradiction in terms. All that God does in Christ He does in free love, moved with compassion for the misery and doom of men. But though God's righteousness as demonstrated in Christ's death—in other words, His action in consistency with His character —includes, and, if we choose to interpret the term properly, even necessitates, the revelation of His grace, it is not this only—I do not believe it is this primarily—which St. Paul has here in mind. God, no doubt, would not do justice to Himself if He did not show His compassion for sinners; but, on the other hand—and here is what the apostle is emphasising—He would not do justice to Himself if He displayed His compassion for sinners in a way which made light of sin, which ignored its tragic reality, or took it for less than it is. In this case He would again be doing Himself injustice; there would be no demonstration that He was true to Himself as the author and guardian of the moral constitution under which men live; as Anselm put it, He would have ceased to be God. The apostle combines the two sides. In Christ set forth a propitiation in His blood—in other words, in the Atonement in which the sinless Son of God enters into the bitter realisation of all that sin means for man, yet loves man under and through it all with an everlasting love—there is an [Greek] *endeixis* of God's righteousness, a demonstration of His self-consistency, in virtue of which we can see how He is at the same time just Himself and the justifier of him who believes on Jesus, a God who is irreconcilable to sin, yet devises means that His banished be not expelled from Him. We may say reverently that this was the only way in which God could forgive. He cannot deny Himself, means at the same time He cannot deny His grace to the sinful, and He cannot deny the moral order in which alone He can live in fellowship with men; and we see the inviolableness of both asserted in the death of Jesus. Nothing else in the world demonstrates how real is God's love to the sinful, and how real the sin of the world is to God. And the love which comes to us through such an expression, bearing sin in all its reality, yet loving us through and beyond it, is the only love which at once forgives and regenerates the soul.

It becomes credible also that there is a *human necessity* for the Atonement: in other words, that apart from it the conditions of being forgiven could no more be fulfilled by man than forgiveness could be bestowed by God.

There are different tendencies in the modern mind with regard to this point. On the one hand, there are those who frankly admit the truth here asserted. Yes, they say, the Atonement is necessary for us. If we are to be saved from our sins, if our hearts are to be touched and won by the love of God, if we are to be emancipated from distrust and reconciled to the Father whose love we have injured, there must be a demonstration of that love so wonderful and overpowering that all pride, alienation and fear shall be overcome by it; and this is what we have in the death of Christ. It is a demonstration of love powerful enough to evoke penitence and faith in man, and it is through penitence and faith alone that man is separated from his sins and reconciled to God. A demonstration of love, too, must be given in act; it is not enough to be told that God loves: the reality of love lies in another region than that of words. In Christ on His cross the very thing itself is present, beyond all hope of telling wonderful, and without its irresistible appeal our hearts could never have been melted to penitence, and won for God. On the other hand, there are those who reject the Atonement on the very ground that for pardon and reconciliation nothing is required but repentance, the assumption being that repentance is something which man can and must produce out of his own resources.

On these divergent tendencies in the modern mind I should wish to make the following remarks.

First, the idea that man can repent as he ought, and whenever he will, without coming under any obligation to God for his repentance, but rather (it might almost be imagined) putting God under obligation by it, is one to which experience lends no support. Repentance is an adequate sense not of our folly, nor of our misery, but of our sin: as the New Testament puts it, it is repentance *toward God*. It is the consciousness of what our sin is to Him: of the wrong it does to His holiness, of the wound which it inflicts on His love. Now such a consciousness it is not in the power of the sinner to produce at will. The more deeply he has sinned, the more (so to speak) repentance is needed, the less is it in his power. It is the very nature of sin to darken the mind and harden the heart, to take away the knowledge of God alike in His holiness and in His love. Hence it is only through a revelation of God, and especially of what God is in relation to sin, that repentance can be evoked in the soul. Of all terms in the vocabulary of religion, repentance is probably the one which is most frequently misused. It is habitually applied to experiences which are not even remotely akin to true penitence. The self-centred regret which a man feels when his sin has found him out—the wish, compounded of pride, shame, and anger at his own inconceivable folly, that he had not done it: these are spoken of as repentance. But they are not repentance at all. They have no relation to God. They constitute no fitness for a new relation to Him. They are no opening of the heart in the direction of His reconciling love. It is the simple truth that that sorrow of heart, that healing and sanctifying pain in which sin is really put away, is not ours in independence of God; it is a saving grace which is begotten in the soul under that impression of sin which it owes to the revelation of God in Christ. A man can no more repent than he can do anything else without a motive, and the motive which makes evangelic repentance possible does not enter into his world till he sees God as God makes Himself known in the death of Christ. All true penitents are children of the Cross. Their penitence is not their own creation: it is the reaction towards God produced in their souls by this demonstration of what sin is to Him, and of what His love does to reach and win the sinful.

The other remark I wish to make refers to those who admit the death of Christ to be necessary *for us*—necessary, in the way I have just described, to evoke penitence and trust in God—but who on this very ground deny it to be *divinely* necessary. It had to be, because the hard hearts of men could not be touched by anything less moving: but that is all. This, I feel sure, is another instance of those false abstractions to which reference has already been made. There is no incompatibility between a *divine* necessity and a necessity *for us*. It may very well be the case that nothing less than the death of Christ could win the trust of sinful men for God, and at the same time that nothing else than the death of Christ could fully reveal the character of God in relation at once to sinners and to sin. For my own part I am persuaded, not only that there is no incompatibility between the two things, but that they are essentially related, and that only the acknowledgment of the divine necessity in Christ's death enables us to conceive in any rational way the power which it exercises over sinners in inducing repentance and faith. It would not evoke a reaction Godward unless God were really present in it, that is, unless it were a real revelation of His being and will: but in a real revelation of God's being and will there can be nothing arbitrary, nothing which is determined only from without, nothing, in other words, that is not divinely necessary. The demonstration of what God is, which is made in the death of Christ, is no doubt a demonstration singularly suited to call forth penitence and faith in man, but the necessity of it does not lie simply in the desire to call forth penitence and faith. It lies in the divine nature itself. God could not do justice to Himself, in relation to man and sin, in any way less awful than this; and it is the fact that He does not shrink even from this—that in the Person of His Son He enters, if we may say so, into the whole responsibility of the situation created by sin—which constitutes the death of Jesus a demonstration of divine love, compelling penitence and faith. Nothing less would have been sufficient to touch sinful hearts to their depths—in that sense the Atonement is humanly necessary; but neither would anything else be a sufficient revelation of what God is in relation to sin and to sinful men—in that sense it is divinely necessary. And the divine necessity is the fundamental one. The power exercised over us by the revelation of God at the Cross is dependent on the fact that the revelation is true—in other words, that it exhibits the real relation of God to sinners and to sin. It is not by calculating what will win us, but by acting in consistency with Himself, that God irresistibly appeals to men. We dare not say that He must be gracious, as though grace could cease to be free: but we may say that He must be Himself, and that it is because He is what we see Him to be in the death of Christ, understood as the New Testament understands it, that sinners are moved to repentance and to trust in Him. That which the eternal being of God made necessary to Him in the presence of sin is the very thing which is necessary also to win the hearts of sinners. Nothing but what is divinely necessary could have met the necessities of sinful men.

When we admit this twofold necessity for the Atonement, we can tell ourselves more clearly how we are to conceive Christ in it, in relation to God on the one hand and to man on the other. The Atonement is God's work. It is God who makes the Atonement in Christ. It is God who mediates His forgiveness of sins to us in this way. This is one aspect of the matter, and probably the one about which there is least dispute among Christians. But there is another aspect of it. The Mediator between God and man is Himself man, Christ Jesus. What is the relation of the man Christ Jesus to those for whom the Atonement is made? What is the proper term to designate, in this atoning work, what He is in relation to them? The doctrine of Atonement current in the Church in the generation preceding our own answered frankly that in His atoning work Christ is our substitute. He comes in our nature, and He comes into our place. He enters into all the responsibilities that sin has created for us, and He does justice to them in His death. He does not deny any of them: He does not take sin as anything less or else than it is to God; in perfect sinlessness He consents even to die, to submit to that awful experience in which the final reaction of God's holiness against sin is expressed. Death was not *His* due: it was something alien to One Who had nothing amiss; but it was our due, and because it was ours He made it His. It was thus that He made Atonement. *He* bore *our* sins. He took to Himself all that they meant, all in which they had involved the world. He died for them, and in so doing acknowledged the sanctity of that order in which sin and death arc indissolubly united. In other words, He did what the human race could not do for itself, yet what had to be done if sinners were to be saved: for how could men be saved if there were not made in humanity an acknowledgment of all that sin is to God, and of the justice of all that is entailed by sin under God's constitution of the world? Such an acknowledgment, as we have just seen, is divinely necessary, and necessary, too, for man, if sin is to be forgiven.

This was the basis of fact on which the substitutionary character of Christ's sufferings and death in the Atonement was asserted. It may be admitted at once that when the term substitute is interpreted without reference to this basis of fact it lends itself very easily to misconstruction. It falls in with, if it does not suggest, the idea of a transference of merit and demerit, the sin of the world being carried over to Christ's account, and the merit of Christ to the world's account, as if the reconciliation of God and man, or the forgiveness of sins and the regeneration of souls, could be explained without the use of higher categories than are employed in bookkeeping. It is surely not necessary at this time of day to disclaim an interpretation of personal relations which makes use only of sub-personal categories. Merit and demerit cannot be mechanically transferred like sums in an account. The credit, so to speak, of one person in the moral sphere cannot become that of another, apart from moral conditions. It is the same truth, in other words, if we say that the figure of paying a debt is not in every respect adequate to describe what Christ does in making the Atonement. The figure, I believe, covers the truth; if it did not, we should not have the kind of language which frequently occurs in Scripture; but it is misread into falsehood and immorality whenever it is pressed as if it were exactly equivalent to the truth. But granting these drawbacks which attach to the word, is there not something in the work of Christ, as mediating the forgiveness of sins, which no other word can express? No matter on what subsequent conditions its virtue for us depends, what Christ did had to be done, or we should never have had forgiveness; we should never have known God, and His nature and will in relation to sin; we should never have had the motive which alone could beget real repentance; we should never have had the spirit which welcomes pardon and is capable of receiving it. We could not procure these things for ourselves, we could not produce them out of our own resources: but He by entering into our nature and lot, by taking on Him our responsibilities and dying our death, has so revealed God to us as to put them within our reach. We owe them to Him; in particular, and in the last resort, we owe them to the fact that He bore our sins in His own body to the tree. If we are not to say that the Atonement, as a work carried through in the sufferings and death of Christ, sufferings and death determined by our sin, is vicarious or substitutionary, what are we to call it?

The only answer which has been given to this question, by those who continue to speak of Atonement at all, is that we must conceive Christ not as the substitute but as the representative of sinners. I venture to think that, with some advantages, the drawbacks of this word are quite as serious as those which attach to substitute. It makes it less easy, indeed, to think of the work of Christ as a finished work which benefits the sinner *ipso facto*, and apart from any relation between him and the Saviour: but of what sort is the relation which it does suggest? It suggests that the sinners who are to be saved by Christ can put Christ forward in their name: they are not in the utterly hopeless case that has hitherto been supposed; they can present themselves to God in the person and work of One on whom God cannot but look with approval. The boldest expression of this I have ever seen occurs in some remarks in the *Primitive Methodist Quarterly Review* on the doctrine of St. Paul. The reviewer is far from saying that a writer who finds a substitutionary doctrine throughout the New Testament is altogether wrong. He goes so far as to admit that 'if we look at the matter from what may be called an external point of view, no doubt we may speak of the death of Christ as in a certain sense substitutionary.' What this 'certain sense' is, he does not define. But no one, he tells us, can do justice to Paul who fails to recognise that the death of Christ was a racial act; and 'if we place ourselves at Paul's point of view, we shall see that to the eye of God the death of Christ presents itself less as an act which Christ does for the race than as an act which the race does in Christ.' In plain English, Paul teaches less that Christ died for the ungodly, than that the ungodly in Christ died for themselves. This is presented to us as something profound, a recognition of the mystical depths in Paul's teaching: I own I can see nothing profound in it except a profound misapprehension of the apostle. Nevertheless, it brings out the logic of what representative means when representative is opposed to substitute. The representative is ours, we are in Him, and we are supposed to get over all the moral difficulties raised by the idea of substitution just because He is ours, and because we are one with Him. But the fundamental fact of the situation is that, to begin with, Christ is *not* ours, and we are *not* one with Him. In the apostle's view, and in point of fact, we are 'without Christ' ([Greek] *chôris Christou*). It is not we who have put Him there. It is not to us that His presence and His work in the world are due. If we had produced Him and put Him forward, we might call Him our representative in the sense suggested by the sentences just quoted; we might say it is not so much He who dies for us, as we who die in Him; but a representative not produced by us, but given to us—not chosen by us, but the elect of God—is not a representative at all, but in that place a substitute. He stands in our stead, facing all our responsibilities for us as God would have them faced; and it is what He does for us, and not the effect which this produces in us, still less the fantastic abstraction of a 'racial act,' which is the Atonement in the sense of the New Testament. To speak of Christ as our representative, in the sense that His death is to God less an act which He does for the race than an act which the race does in Him, is in principle to deny the

43

whole grace of the gospel, and to rob it of every particle of its motive power.

To do justice to the truth here, both on its religious and its ethical side, it is necessary to put in their proper relation to one another the aspects of reality which the terms substitute and representative respectively suggest. The first is fundamental. Christ is God's gift to humanity. He stands in the midst of us, the pledge of God's love, accepting our responsibilities as God would have them accepted, offering to God, under the pressure of the world's sin and all its consequences, that perfect recognition of God's holiness in so visiting sin which men should have offered but could not; and in so doing He makes Atonement for us. In so doing, also, He is our substitute, not yet our representative. But the Atonement thus made is not a spectacle, it is a motive. It is not a transaction in business, or in book-keeping, which is complete in itself; in view of the relations of God and man it belongs to its very nature to be a moral appeal. It is a divine challenge to men, which is designed to win their hearts. And when men are won—when that which Christ in His love has done for them comes home to their souls—when they are constrained by His infinite grace to the self-surrender of faith, then we may say He becomes their representative. They begin to feel that what He has done for them must not remain outside of them, but be reproduced somehow in their own life. The mind of Christ in relation to God and sin, as He bore their sins in His own body to the tree, must become their mind; this and nothing else is the Christian salvation. The power to work this change in them is found in the death of Christ itself; the more its meaning is realised as something there, in the world, outside of us, the more completely does it take effect within us. In proportion as we see and feel that out of pure love to us He stands in our place —our substitute—bearing our burden—in that same proportion are we drawn into the relation to Him that makes Him our representative. But we should be careful here not to lose ourselves in soaring words. The New Testament has much to say about union with Christ, but I could almost be thankful that it has no such expression as mystical union. The only union it knows is a moral one —a union due to the moral power of Christ's death, operating morally as a constraining motive on the human will, and begetting in believers the mind of Christ in relation to sin; but this moral union remains the problem and the task, as well as the reality and the truth, of the Christian life. Even when we think of Christ as our representative, and have the courage to say we died with Him, we have still to *reckon* ourselves to be dead to sin, and to *put to death* our members which are upon the earth; and to go past this, and speak of a mystical union with Christ in which we are lifted above the region of reflection and motive, of gratitude and moral responsibility, into some kind of metaphysical identity with the Lord, does not promote intelligibility, to say the least. If the Atonement were not, to begin with, outside of us—if it were not in that sense objective, a finished work in which God in Christ makes a final revelation of Himself in relation to sinners and sin—in other words, if Christ could not be conceived in it as our substitute, given by God to do in our place what we could not do for ourselves, there would be no way of recognising or preaching or receiving it as a motive; while, on the other hand, if it did not operate as a motive, if it did not appeal to sinful men in such a way as to draw them into a moral fellowship with Christ—in other words, if Christ did not under it become representative of us, our surety to God that we should yet be even as He in relation to God and to sin, we could only say that it had all been vain. Union with Christ, in short, is not a presupposition of Christ's work, which enables us to escape all the moral problems raised by the idea of a substitutionary Atonement; it is not a presupposition of Christ's work, it is its fruit. To see that it is its fruit is to have the final answer to the objection that substitution is immoral. If substitution, in the sense in which we must assert it of Christ, is the greatest moral force in the world—if the truth which it covers, when it enters into the mind of man, enters with divine power to assimilate him to the Saviour, uniting him to the Lord in a death to sin and a life to God—obviously, to call it immoral is an abuse of language. The love which can literally go out of itself and make the burden of others its own is the radical principle of all the genuine and victorious morality in the world. And to say that love cannot do any such thing, that the whole formula of morality is, every man shall bear his own burden, is to deny the plainest facts of the moral life.

Yet this is a point at which difficulty is felt by many in trying to grasp the Atonement. On the one hand, there do seem to be analogies to it, and points of attachment for it, in experience. No sin that has become real to conscience is ever outlived and overcome without expiation. There are consequences involved in it that go far beyond our perception at the moment, but they work themselves inexorably out, and our sin ceases to be a burden on conscience, and a fetter on will, only as we 'accept the punishment of our iniquity,' and become conscious of the holy love of God behind it. But the consequences of sin are never limited to the sinner. They spread beyond him in the organism of humanity, and when they strike visibly upon the innocent, the sense of guilt is deepened. We see that we have done we know not what, something deeply and mysteriously bad beyond all our reckoning, something that only a power and goodness transcending our own avail to check. It is one of the startling truths of the moral life that such consequences of sin, striking visibly upon the innocent, have in certain circumstances a peculiar power to redeem the sinful. When they are accepted, as they sometimes are accepted, without repining or complaint—when they are borne, as they sometimes are borne, freely and lovingly by the innocent, because to the innocent the guilty are dear—then something is appealed to in the guilty which is deeper than guilt, something may be touched which is deeper than sin, a new hope and faith may be born in them, to take hold of love so wonderful, and by attaching themselves to it to transcend the evil past. The suffering of such love (they are dimly aware), or rather the power of such love persisting through all the suffering brought on it by sin, opens the gate of righteousness to the sinful in spite of all that has been; sin is outweighed by it, it is annulled, exhausted, transcended in it. The great Atonement of Christ is somehow in line with this, and we do not need to shrink from the analogy. 'If there were no witness,' as Dr. Robertson Nicoll puts it, 'in the world's deeper literature'—if there were no witness, that is, in the universal experience of man—'to the fact of an Atonement, the Atonement would be useless, since the formula expressing it would be unintelligible.' It is the analogy of such experiences which makes the Atonement credible, yet it must always in some way transcend them. There is something in it which is ultimately incomparable. When we speak of others as innocent, the term is used only in a relative sense; there is no human conscience pure to God. When we speak of the sin of others coming in its consequences on the innocent, we speak of something in which the innocent are purely passive; if there is moral response on their part, the situation is not due to moral initiative of theirs. But with Christ it is different. He knew *no* sin, and He entered *freely*, deliberately, and as the very work of His calling, into all that sin meant for God and brought on man. Something that I experience in a particular relation, in which another has borne my sin and loved me through it, may help to open my eyes to the meaning of Christ's love; but when they are opened, what I see is the propitiation for the whole world. There is no guilt of the human race, there is no consequence in which sin has involved it, to which the holiness and love made manifest in Christ are unequal. He reveals to all sinful men the whole relation of God to them and to their sins—a sanctity which is inexorable to sin, and cannot take it as other than it is in all its consequences, and a love which through all these consequences and under the weight of them all, will not let the sinful go. It is in this revelation of the character of God and of His relation to the sin of the world that the forgiveness of sins is revealed. It is not intimated in the air; it is preached, as St. Paul says, 'in this man'; it is mediated to the world through Him and specifically through His death, because it is through Him, and specifically through His death, that we get the knowledge of God's character which evokes penitence and faith, and brings the assurance of His pardon to the heart.

From this point of view we may see how to answer the question that is sometimes asked about the relation of Christ's life to His death, or about the relation of both to the Atonement. If we say that what we have in the

Atonement is an assurance of God's character, does it not follow at once that Christ's teaching and His life contribute to it as directly as His death? Is it not a signal illustration of the false abstractions which we have so often had cause to censure, when the death of Christ is taken as if it had an existence or a significance apart from His life, or could be identified with the Atonement in a way in which His life could not? I do not think this is so clear. Of course it is Christ Himself who is the Atonement or propitiation—He Himself, as St. John puts it, and not anything, not even His death, into which He does not enter. But it is He Himself, as making to us the revelation of God in relation to sin and to sinners; and apart from death, as that in which the conscience of the race sees the final reaction of God against evil, this revelation is not fully made. If Christ had done less than die for us, therefore—if He had separated Himself from us, or declined to be one with us, in the solemn experience in which the darkness of sin is sounded and all its bitterness tasted,—there would have been no Atonement. It is impossible to say this of any particular incident in His life, and in so far the unique emphasis laid on His death in the New Testament is justified. But I should go further than this, and say that even Christ's life, taking it as it stands in the Gospels, only enters into the Atonement, and has reconciling power, because it is pervaded from beginning to end by the consciousness of His death. Instead of depriving His death of the peculiar significance Scripture assigns to it, and making it no more than the termination, or at least the consummation, of His life, I should rather argue that the Scriptural emphasis is right, and that His life attains its true interpretation only as we find in it everywhere the power and purpose of His death. There is nothing artificial or unnatural in this. There are plenty of people who never have death out of their minds an hour at a time. They are not cowards, nor mad, nor even sombre: they may have purposes and hopes and gaieties as well as others; but they see life steadily and see it whole, and of all their thoughts the one which has most determining and omnipresent power is the thought of the inevitable end. There is death in all their life. It was not, certainly, as the inevitable end, the inevitable 'debt of nature,' that death was present to the mind of Christ; but if we can trust the Evangelists at all, from the hour of His baptism it was present to His mind as something involved in His vocation; and it was a presence so tremendous that it absorbed everything into itself. 'I have a baptism to be baptized with, and how am I straitened till it be accomplished.' Instead of saying that Christ's life as well as His death contributed to the Atonement—that His active obedience (to use the theological formula) as well as His passive obedience was essential to His propitiation—we should rather say that His life is part of His death: a deliberate and conscious descent, ever deeper and deeper, into the dark valley where at the last hour the last reality of sin was to be met and borne. And if the objection is made that after all this only means that death is the most vital point of life, its intensest focus, I should not wish to make any reply. Our Lord's Passion *is* His sublimest action—an action so potent that all His other actions are sublated in it, and we know everything when we know that He *died* for our sins.

The desire to bring the life of Christ as well as His death into the Atonement has probably part of its motive in the feeling that when the death is separated from the life it loses moral character: it is reduced to a merely physical incident, which cannot carry such vast significance as the Atonement. Such a feeling certainly exists, and finds expression in many forms. How often, for example, we hear it said that it is not the death which atones, but the spirit in which the Saviour died—not His sufferings which expiate sin, but the innocence, the meekness, the love to man and obedience to God in which they were borne. The Atonement, in short, was a moral achievement, to which physical suffering and death are essentially irrelevant. This is our old enemy, the false abstraction, once more, and that in the most aggressive form. The contrast of physical and moral is made absolute at the very point at which it ceases to exist. As against such absolute distinctions we must hold that if Christ had not really died for us, there would have been no Atonement at all, and on the other hand that what are called His physical sufferings and death have no existence simply as physical: they are essential elements in the moral achievement of the passion. It leads to no truth to say that it is not His death, but the spirit in which He died, that atones for sin: the spirit in which He died has its being in His death, and in nothing else in the world.

It seems to me that what is really wanted here, both by those who seek to co-ordinate Christ's life with His death in the Atonement, and by those who distinguish between His death and the spirit in which He died, is some means of keeping hold of the Person of Christ in His work, and that this is not effectively done apart from the New Testament belief in the Resurrection. There is no doubt that in speaking of the death of Christ as that through which the forgiveness of sins is mediated to us we are liable to think of it as if it were only an event in the past. We take the representation of it in the Gospel and say, "Such and such is the impression which this event produces upon me; I feel in it how God is opposed to sin, and how I ought to be opposed to it; I feel in it how God's love appeals to me to share His mind about sin; and as I yield to this appeal I am at once set free from sin and assured of pardon; this is the only ethical forgiveness; to know this experimentally is to know the Gospel." No one can have any interest in disputing another's obligation to Christ, but it may fairly be questioned whether this kind of obligation to Christ amounts to Christianity in the sense of the New Testament. There is no living Christ here, no coming of the living Christ to the soul, in the power of the Atonement, to bring it to God. But this is what the New Testament shows us. It is *He* who is the propitiation for our sins—He who died for them and rose again. The New Testament preaches a Christ who was dead and is alive, not a Christ who was alive and is dead. It is a mistake to suppose that the New Testament conception of the Gospel, involving as it does the spiritual presence and action of Christ, in the power of the Atonement, is a matter of indifference to us, and that in all our thinking and preaching we must remain within purely historical limits, if by purely historical limits is meant that our creed must end with the words "crucified, dead, and buried." To preach the Atonement means not only to preach One who bore our sins in death, but One who by rising again from the dead demonstrated the final defeat of sin, and One who comes in the power of His risen life—which means, in the power of the Atonement accepted by God—to make all who commit themselves to Him in faith partakers in His victory. It is not His death, as an incident in the remote past, however significant it may be; it is the Lord Himself, appealing to us in the virtue of His death, who assures us of pardon and restores our souls.

One of the most singular phenomena in the attitude of many modern minds to the Atonement is the disposition to plead against the Atonement what the New Testament represents as its fruits. It is as though it had done its work so thoroughly that people could not believe that it ever needed to be done at all. The idea of fellowship with Christ, for example, is constantly urged against the idea that Christ died for us, and by His death made all mankind His debtors in a way in which we cannot make debtors of each other. The New Testament itself is pressed into the service. It is pointed out that our Lord called His disciples to drink of His cup and to be baptized with His baptism, where the baptism and the cup are figures of His passion; and it is argued that there cannot be anything unique in His experience or service, anything which He does for men which it is beyond the power of His disciples to do also. Or again, reference is made to St. Paul's words to the Colossians: 'Now I rejoice in my sufferings on your behalf, and fill up on my part that which is lacking of the afflictions of Christ in my flesh for His body's sake, which is the Church'; and it is argued that St. Paul here represents himself as doing exactly what Christ did, or even as supplementing a work which Christ admittedly left imperfect. The same idea is traced where the Christian is represented as called into the fellowship of the Son of God, or more specifically as called to know the fellowship of His sufferings by becoming conformed to His death. It is seen pervading the New Testament in the conception of the Christian as a man *in Christ*. And to descend from the apostolic age to our own, it has been put by an American theologian into the epigrammatic form that Christ redeems us by making us redeemers. What, it may be asked, is the truth in all this? and how is it related to what we have already seen cause to assert about the uniqueness of Christ's work in making atonement for sin, or mediating the divine forgiveness to man?

I do not think it is impossible or even difficult to reconcile the two: it is done, indeed, whenever we see that the life to which we are summoned, in the fellowship of Christ, is a life which we owe altogether to Him, and which He does not in the least owe to us. The question really raised is this: Has Jesus Christ a place of His own in the Christian religion? Is it true that there is one Mediator between God and man, Himself man, this man, Christ Jesus? In spite of the paradoxical assertion of Harnack to the contrary, it is not possible to deny, with any plausibility, that this was the mind of Christ Himself, and that it has been the mind of all who call Him Lord. He knew and taught, what they have learned by experience as well as by His word, that all men must owe to Him their knowledge of the Father, their place in the Kingdom of God, and their part in all its blessings. He could not have taught this of any but Himself, nor is it the experience of the Church that such blessings come through any other. Accordingly, when Christ calls on men to drink His cup and to be baptized with His baptism, while He may quite well mean, and does mean, that His life and death are to be the inspiration of theirs, and while He may quite well encourage them to believe that sacrifice on their part, as on His, will contribute to bless the world, He need not mean, and we may be sure He does not mean, that their blood is, like His, the blood of the covenant, or that their sinful lives, even when purged and quickened by His Spirit, could be, like His sinless life, described as the world's ransom. The same considerations apply to the passages quoted from St. Paul, and especially to the words in Colossians i. 24. The very purpose of the Epistle to the Colossians is to assert the exclusive and perfect mediatorship of Christ, alike in creation and redemption; all that we call being, and all that we call reconciliation, has to be defined by relation to Him, and not by relation to any other persons or powers, visible or invisible; and however gladly Paul might reflect that in his enthusiasm for suffering he was continuing Christ's work, and exhausting some of the afflictions—they were Christ's own afflictions— which had yet to be endured ere the Church could be made perfect, it is nothing short of grotesque to suppose that in this connection he conceived of himself as doing what Christ did, atoning for sin, and reconciling the world to God. All this was done already, perfectly done, done for the whole world; and it was on the basis of it, and under the inspiration of it, that the apostle sustained his enthusiasm for a life of toil and pain in the service of men.

Always, where we have Christian experience to deal with, it is the Christ through whom the divine forgiveness comes to us at the Cross—the Christ of the substitutionary Atonement, who bore all our burden alone, and did a work to which we can for ever recur, but to which we did not and do not and never can contribute at all—it is this Christ who constrains us to find our representative with God in Himself, and to become ourselves His representatives to men. It is as we truly represent Him that we can expect our testimony to Him to find acceptance, but that testimony far transcends everything that our service enables men to measure. What is anything that a sinful man, saved by grace, can do for his Lord or for his kind, compared with what the sinless Lord has done for the sinful race? It is true that He calls us to drink of His cup, to learn the fellowship of His sufferings, even to be conformed to His death; but under all the intimate relationship the eternal difference remains which makes Him *Lord*—He knew no sin, and we could make no atonement. It is the goal of our life to be found in Him; but I cannot understand the man who thinks it more profound to identify himself with Christ and share in the work of redeeming the world, than to abandon himself to Christ and share in the world's experience of being redeemed. And I am very sure that in the New Testament the last is first and fundamental.